Rose

A story from Tanzania

Adrian Strain

This book is dedicated to friends and colleagues in Mtwara, Tanzania and the residents of the small district of Kiangu. Mr Philibert Ngairo and Mr Abdulmajid Sabil should be thanked especially for their friendship and their advice,

Chapter One

Rose woke as usual at around five o'clock. She lay there for a few moments, thinking about the conversation she'd had last night with her grandfather. She said her morning prayer, called to her young sister to wake up, then prised herself from her bed. Her grandfather had been telling a story of their family. It was a long, complicated story that seemed to have no end, no purpose. It was a story that had many twists and turns and, it being her grandfather, had no way of being verified. In the end, she'd begged him to let her go to bed.

It had been this way for as long as she could remember. Her grandfather, Babu Jackson – as every African for perhaps forty kilometres knew him – told outlandish stories, stories that you knew were not wholly true, but that fixed you to your spot just in case there was some truth hidden there that you might miss. That would be foolish and everyone would know you to be a fool. So, you listened – fixed – and laughed, then exhaled loudly, then tutted your teeth, then laughed again as you wiped away tears from your face.

Last night had been no different. He told a story of the great Shaka and the days when African tribes were at war with each other. His great grandfather, although not a Zulu, had, through happenstance, found himself marching northwards in Shaka's great domination.

Shaka's soldiers had moved north for month after month and Babu Jackson's ancestor, Mtumbi, part British, had at first been prisoner then enlisted to prepare food and carry supplies.

One night as the soldiers slept, Mtumbi had been disturbed by the peculiar shriek of a leopard. The sound came from some reddish rocks peppering the bush at a low ridge some hundred meters away. Mtumbi had collected his few belongings and run for cover in the bush. He crouched and listened as the shrieks became louder; he knew he should warn his fellows and as he saw the shadows of the leopard enlarged in the light of the fires burning through the night, he ran, waving his arms madly and kicking up dirt as hard as he could. The leopard stopped, looked and turned nonchalantly away. When soldiers woke with the dawn, one told of his dream, of a leopard and a great struggle. Mtumbi was thrilled when he realised that his heroic struggle with the leopard had been of such importance that it had entered the soldier's dreams. The soldiers believed Mtumbi to be both a hero and modest. Such heroic stories and other tales of woe and foolishness litter their family's history.

Rose, maintained Babu Jackson, should be ready always to take advantage. His story complete, at least for tonight, Jackson had kissed Rose noisily as he left the house, laughing too loudly for little ones to sleep, risking a sharp word from sisters and cousins nursing their little ones close by.

She'd slept badly, waking often and dreaming so vividly that at one point she tried to force herself to stay awake. In her fitful dozing, she'd dreamt of the old crooked man her grandfather had described, his goat that could sing beautiful old songs and a baby that turned into a snake. She had woken trembling.

There was a time when she was often frightened but a restless night such as the one from which she'd just woken was now a rarity. Why did she used to have such dreams? Nothing in her life should have made her any different from her friends. She had no-one with whom she could talk and exchange such private thoughts and her mother would shoo her away like a wasp had she bothered her with such nonsense.

Eventually, although her eyes still stung, she stretched her toes, went outside to urinate, came inside, washed her face in a plastic bowl of cold water, put on her maroon skirt and freshly washed white blouse for school and went into the living room to greet her mother. The hens were to be let out and some scraps thrown for their feed. They squawked and fought over the scraps and the rooster started his ritual of chasing a younger hen, grabbing it by the neck with a scabby yellowed beak and with wings flapping, dust flying and the most ear-piercing commotion, forced itself on the defenceless bird.

The sky was a warm grey, lightening to a pale blue. Before Rose got to school it would be hot and white and bright. The ground was parched and dusty and cracked, but still it must be swept and cleaned. She took the small besom from behind the door and bent low to sweep the loose dirt that had gathered overnight. She was barefoot, to keep her white socks clean for school. She went back inside, drank as quickly as she could the plastic cup of weak porridge her mother had prepared, checked her books were in order in her school bag, kissed her mother on the cheek and ran down the hill to catch her friends. They had a forty-minute walk to school and there was much to talk about.

Rose was tall with pale skin. She had a wiry build with close cropped hair and an angular jaw. She shared her mother's habit of looking nervously – suspiciously – when first approached. In her mother's case, this was probably learned behaviour from the abuse she suffered as a child, but in Rose's case it belied an inner confidence which showed itself in her straight back, broad smile and loud voice. She had a long stride and her friend skipped every few steps to keep up.

The town of Mbulu was just waking up as it did every morning when the sun popped its head over the line of trees at the edge of town and started heating up the tin roofs. Mr Ali was opening his small shop and setting out cartons of bottled water. Nailed to the wooden boards he used to close his shop at night were tea-bags held together with a long line of cotton. His shop sold toothpaste, soap, razor blades, sweets, small bottles of coloured soda, so brightly coloured they looked like some chemistry magician's supplies. He sold small tube-shaped bricks of red soil, favoured by many women for their digestion. Some believed it could help them conceive. He sold tiny sachets of white powder for killing rats, and great grey blocks of soap for washing clothes. He sold brushes and buckets, shoe laces and polish and cheap Chinese batteries. His wife, Sharifa, would sit in the dark cool at the rear of the shop, almost hidden by the paraphernalia hanging around her. She would cook rice for her husband and serve it to him when he returned from prayers, when she would return to her vigil, watching young children playing outside and flicking flies from her counter.

Mama Ntile was waddling by, her great fat thighs, slapping and chafing under the billowing drape of a robe she wore most days. She went barefoot in the morning; her feet, like a plasterer's board, padded their way through the dust and dirt and only when she arrived at the Commissioner's office would she squeeze on her shoes, too tight and too dear to wear. She was an Assistant Administrative Officer which meant that she typed up notices as dictated to her or written down for her by Mr Jin, the Administrative Officer. She had been trained in the use of the computer at a workshop last year, where Mr Jin got drunk and asked to sleep with her. She could now use the word processor and the printer.

Mbulu's district offices were situated behind the big bus station and next to the great concrete bulk of St Paul's Catholic Church. The church had been built with European money but had used local trades and consequently it boasted modern strip lighting but with brackets that dangled precariously from the loose plaster. It was, nevertheless, one of the most lavishly appointed buildings in Mbulu, second only to the District Commissioner's residence.

As the girls arrived at school, the clanging of the great iron wheel swinging from the baobab tree called students to gather and line up, ready for the school assembly. Nothing was said. Five teachers with the headteacher in the centre, took up their positions on the patch of ground immediately in front of the office and the staff room. The morning sun was already high and hot enough to make the shade of the school an obvious haven, compared with the baked ground where the four hundred or so pupils were now gathering.

One small boy, barefoot and in shirt and shorts only, beat a drum and one older girl, in maroon shirt and white shirt, sang the opening line of the national anthem. The second line and the remainder of the song was sung by the whole school, older boys offering a tenor harmony. Although the song was sung beautifully, the children's faces were expressionless. This daily routine had ceased to move their souls a long time ago.

The duties of the day were called out by a boy in the front line; the headteacher stepped forward and made some remarks about the forthcoming monthly tests. He reminded class monitors to make sure that the classes for which they were responsible complete their cleaning duties properly. As the school assembly splintered into small groups of students meandering to their classrooms, the second master stepped forward with a long stick broken from a nearby bush and read out a litany of nine names, boys and girls. Without a word between them, but with nervous dark looks and heads hung in anticipation, they moved away from their line and clustered in front of the teacher. He barked and they immediately crouched on their haunches. One girl started whimpering and, as her colleague pulled her down by her skirt, she started wailing, then screaming. The teacher took one step and lashed her calves with the stick. She yelped, then fell silent and crouched. Another barked instruction and the straggly group formed a scruffy line. Starting at one end, each first grimaced, then held out their right arm stiffly, fingers stretched, as the teacher, with a short jerk of the lower arm, brought the stick down across their trembling fingers. As the stick came down, their arms flinched, the wounded hand was grabbed instantly by its left neighbour, faces scrunched, mouths gaped and in some cases, tears were squeezed from eyes clenched shut.

As the line of punishment came to an end, the group dispersed. No-one spoke. One girl whimpered; others looked at their hands to see if the pain would show itself in a weal or a burn – but all moved slowly to their respective classrooms. One young man, Innocent, stuffed his hands deep into his pockets. His trousers bulged and strained but he would not let the pain in his fingers betray him. As he took up his seat at the back of the classroom, Rose turned to smile but he looked away, winked at one of his friends and took out his exercise book.

Innocent was a year or two older than many of the other students. It wasn't clear how his school fees were paid or if they were paid but he came from a poor home and his clothes and basic school equipment could not hide it. He'd arrived in school in Form I, knowing no-one. He was not from Mbulu and Rose had not seen him in villages or village events. He appeared one day, a foot taller than most, with a wide grin, a jet-black skin and huge tough feet that could kick a ball or a boy's shins harder than anyone else.

The chalkboard was covered with neat spidery writing, divided into three columns and with paragraphs neatly spaced with underlinings. There was no teacher to help them; she was sitting in the staffroom, marking exercise books and chatting about the President's speech which so many people were talking about. Promises of an end to corruption, greater food security and more jobs for young people had all been heard before. None of the teachers in this school believed it. But it was better to listen to those empty promises than sit in an airless room with sixty students.

As a young girl, Rose would lie in bed constructing very detailed pictures of herself in a white coat, sometimes wearing glasses, smiling at a photographer. The young woman alongside the article entitled, "Why your daughter should study science", stood proudly, smiling, surrounded by taller, older men. The article required patriotic parents to think about their family and their nation's future before allowing their daughter to be married young and have babies. The country needed scientists. A white hot technological revolution will create a generation of white-coated girls with perfect white teeth. Your daughter should be amongst them. ....

Rose's interest in science was nurtured by the arrival of a young teacher, a nun from a nearby convent. Sister Raphael was a slight woman of indeterminate age, the only signs being the few grey hairs springing from beneath her veil. She was admired and respected by most pupils simply because she took an obvious pleasure in being in their company. When a student needed to speak to her she would stop her marking of exercise books and leap with enthusiasm to see how she could help; she led choir twice a week after school, catch-up classes in English and was one of the few teachers in school to know and remember the names of every pupil.

The school had no science equipment. It had a classroom designated as a science laboratory; it had large desks with redundant gas taps and stools rather than chairs, but test tubes, and glass beakers had long ago been locked in cupboards behind the teacher's dais, next to the cracked chalkboard. Despite the absence of equipment, Sister Raphael taught her class science as part of their General Knowledge. They would not be examined in this subject but for those wishing to broaden their minds and gain invaluable background information for the essays they would need to write in History, English and geography, then her General Knowledge catch-up classes each Wednesday afternoon would be useful. Rose loved it. They studied the life cycle of insects and took care drawing labelled diagrams; they studied the fertilisation of plants, the composition of a volcano and the principles of electricity. Sister Raphael had the ability to make every student feel that what they were learning they would need to put to good use any day soon.

Babu Jackson, her grandfather, had talked to her about so many things; stories of the great history of this country; wars, great cruelties, or natural disasters. It seemed at one time that everything important she knew, she knew only because her grandfather had told her. He had been a soldier – first in the European war, then later, for independence and later still in the new republic's army. He wore each uniform with pride. He had met Rose's grandmother while stationed near the border, ready and waiting for incursions. He had wooed her with a crease in his shirt and shiny shoes each day. Anna was their only child. They had three altogether, but two had died as babies.

Anna grew up as a quiet nervous child; she was a burden to her family and she was often reminded of this in looks and words. She lived a lonely existence in such a busy village and when a young soldier came around, Anna was soon distracted. She became pregnant to the first man who paid her attention outside her family. Jacline, was the result of that brief fling, the young man leaving town before he could be told the news of Anna's pregnancy. Rose was the result of a second unhappy union. Her father had demanded marriage or at least money, but the boy's father died whilst the dispute raged on and the young man had disappeared.

Rose's grandfather, cold and uncommunicative with his own daughter, took a great interest in Rose as soon as she was born. He had featured big and bold throughout her childhood. He advised her, he scolded her and he told her stories; some she believed, others she knew he made up. He liked to tell stories; he would get more excited than her sometimes, obviously not being quite sure how the story would end until he got there himself. When she was small there was usually a monkey or a baboon that had lost its mother; as she grew older, it was perhaps a wicked boy who was stolen in the night and now she was regaled with tall tales of his escapades in one army or another.

Throughout the whole of Forms I and II Rose had thought Innocent nothing more than a tiresome boy who like many boys was interested only in being the centre of attention. If such boys were punished or better still removed from school it would be better for those students who wanted to take advantage of the education on offer. She once complained to Sister Raphael,

"But Sister, such boys waste all of our time. Why do they come to school at all? They would do better for their families if they worked in the fields."
"Don't be so harsh, Rose. Innocent will in time come to see the benefits of learning. We don't all grow up at the same time."

Rose didn't see why Sister Raphael was so patient. There were too many students in school and her life would be a lot easier if there were fewer noisy ones in her class.

In Form III, Rose had started to think about Innocent differently. She had been sent to the market one

Saturday morning and was walking home, carrying a basket of food and household items confidently on her head. Innocent was sitting on a veranda outside a men's hairdressers. As she walked passed, smiling and calling out a greeting to him, he jumped up and ran to her side.

"Rose! My flower." His insolence shocked her. Who was he to think he should talk to her in such a way. She walked on, ignoring him. Innocent realising his mistake tried to recover ground.
"It's just a saying. Your name is the name of an English flower. You would know that being so much better than me at English."
"I only know what the rest of the class knows. If you listened more and talked less, you'd know this."

By Form IV, Rose started to think of Innocent more and more. The physical changes in her had coincided with a growing interest in Innocent's appearance. In the last year, he'd grown a little taller but a lot broader in his chest. When he removed his shirt during the cleanliness period – something he was strictly forbidden to do – she noticed the sheen of the sweat on his upper arms and the curve of his back and his buttocks. The shape of him pleased her. He came to some of the catch-up classes with Sister Raphael and walked home with Rose after school. They would talk of all the things Rose wanted to do. She hoped her grandfather would pay for her to continue with her studies into Forms V and VI and she would then be able to go to college and perhaps university, after which she would get a good job as a doctor or a health inspector.

Innocent laughed but asked lots of questions because he liked the sound of her voice and he lacked the confidence to speak so openly about himself. He could make stories up about playing football for Manchester United or Barcelona when he was with other boys, but with Rose he couldn't talk so freely. He seemed to lose the words and so he preferred to listen to her. She loved the fact that he would listen and ask more questions and never seem to tire of hearing all about her. They started meeting as often as studies and discretion would allow. In school Innocent would find pretexts for being close to Rose and sometimes, in front of other boys, wink or say something intended for Rose to find insolent. Rose knew and loved it.

Later that evening, after she had finished her chores and her school work, Rose crept out. Saying only a word to her sister, Jacline, she ran in the dark to the other end of the huddle of houses; a low moon shed a cold light while she waited in the shadow of a clump of small trees. The night was alive with frogs croaking from a nearby pond. Dogs whining for food and cicadas humming added to the ominous atmosphere.

She heard him on his new phone before she saw him, "Yep. Cool. No. Not him." A pause while he listened, then

"Have you got the money? What? Good. Yeah. I'm here now. Yeah. I'll wait."

Rose stepped out of the shadow and Innocent put away his phone.

"Hi, Rose. Finished your studies?"

"I'm here, aren't I? Who were you talking to? And how did you get that phone? Has someone lent you some money? Did you steal it?"

"What! Steal? Is that what you think? That was a guy I need to see."

"I thought you wanted to see me. I'll go back if you're too busy."

"No, baby. I'll only be a few minutes. He will be here right now and then I am yours."

Rose already knew well enough that 'right now' could mean anything. Still, she was too excited at the idea of standing with him for her to remain angry for long. She still had the shortness of breath from running across the village which had now become the sheer thrill of being with Innocent.

He stood facing her, looking down into her face with a look which he hoped showed confidence and superiority. He was a lot taller than Rose and as he smiled he stroked the nape of her neck, his large bony hands covering her rounded shoulders easily. She felt safer than she had ever done in her life; and even though she knew his smile meant nothing, a magnetism triggered a smile from her and he rubbed her cheek with his thumb and bent his head to kiss her. He bit her lip gently, just hard enough for her to recoil slightly.

"This guy I'm meeting has a good business deal for me to consider. It could be good for me." Rose noted and couldn't help resenting his use of the first person. He never used 'us' only 'me'.

"What do you mean? Business deal? You're studying for your exams, aren't you?"

She felt a flicker of nervousness cross her chest. Every possible change to their circumstances she saw as a threat to the future she saw for the two of them. She only referred to it as love in her head. Part of her knew it wasn't really love, but for ease of argument with herself she called it love – for shorthand. But right now, when he talked of 'business', her first thought was him not sitting behind her in class, not meeting him in the shadows before bed, him not planning his future with her as she did with him.

"Don't worry baby. If I get the opening this guy is talking about, I won't need school or certificates."

A flash of anger like a whip cracking, crossed her and she lashed out.

"So, you're already better than that are you. You think you're too clever for school?"

"School? Certificates? What will it get you? A job picking your teeth in an office full of papers and drawers and stamps where things get lost; where the only thing to do is to watch people queue and whine they haven't got a job like yours."

She regretted speaking even before she'd finished her sentence and as Innocent spat out his reply, she realised that there was another brittle side to him that she rarely saw. She loved the boy with the smile, the hand flips and the swagger. Here was an angry young man she knew little about.

And then, as quickly, there he was, with a grin like blood-red melon, his eyes in mock supplication,
"But let's not argue. Baby. Awww." And he took her hand, then held her round shoulder in his basket of a hand and rubbed her cheek some more with his bony thumb. Rose quivered inside, but smiled; then smiled inside. All was well again.

A young man, slightly shorter than Innocent, but probably two years older, approached from the direction of the other village. She had not seen him until he was very close as he had walked in the shadows of the tall trees marking the path linking the two hamlets. The moon was still low and it threw a stark guilty light on their faces.
"How is it Mr Challes? Eh? How are things with you, bwana?"

Innocent was suddenly a young man who knew how to greet a potential business colleague, who was also a potential enemy. Don't show too much smile. Don't show too much frown. Don't show too much.
"OK man. How is it with you? How's the family? How is school? How are things?"

"Fine. Beautiful. Everything is perfect. Let's not talk about school, eh?"

And he turned and winked at Rose like he'd winked at Jerry in class earlier that day, after his beating. She knew it was for anyone who saw it except her. It wasn't for her for, as he winked, he turned and put an arm around Challes' shoulder. Challes looked at the long thin arm as though it were a sticky insect that he should brush away; but in the end, he let it go and they moved a few paces away to plan their next move. Rose stood and tried not to care. She turned to pace towards the edge of the village, towards the start of the first shamba, filled with the short flimsy shoots of this year's maize. There had been rain four or five weeks ago and that had been enough to bring on this early growth, but since then, nothing; and people were already talking about a poor harvest.

Challes and Innocent were getting louder as they slapped each other's hands, laughed louder than they needed and sealed what looked like a very good deal.

"So, I'll see you in Dar next week?" Challes was testing Innocent.

"Do not worry, man. I'll be there." As Challes walked away with a nonchalant wave of his arm above his head, Innocent waited and watched. He turned away as soon as Challes disappeared into the shadows. He faced Rose with exaggerated drooping lips and the flesh below his eyes pulled down,

"What's the matter? Aren't you pleased?"

Rose turned towards home and Innocent wrapped his arm around her waist roughly. In one movement, he could turn her with one arm and the other hold her chin and bend his head to kiss her. Rose felt weak. Angry, but weak.

"You know this is not the way Innocent."

"Rose, baby, you know nothing. You know about history and science and such, but really, you know nothing. You think that those precious exams are going to solve all your problems."

"But what about school? What will you tell them? Shall I tell Ngonyani? He will be so disappointed."

"Are you kidding? He cares about you and his other goody-goodies. Do you seriously think he'll give a second thought to me not being there? One seat going spare. One less book to mark."

"Maybe not, but…"

"Stop! We shouldn't argue tonight." And he pulled her towards him. "I'll leave for Dar tomorrow morning."

She felt herself, like soft sand, heated and dried by the white sun, slipping to fill the space around her. His body was the only solid thing in her world and her fluid shifting body became shapeless around him. She could feel him pressing against her and she was able with what seemed like the last act of will in her body to step away from him, remove the kanga from around her waist and lay it on the ground at their feet. Their lovemaking was silent and uncomfortable; finished quickly and, afterwards, an awkward silence fell between them. Innocent got up and walked a short distance from her to allow her to arrange her clothing.

As Innocent moved away, Rose felt empty. She wondered if he would call her from Dar; she wondered what would happen to him when he was alone in that great sprawling place. She had never been far from her village in all her sixteen years – just once travelling to a village some kilometres away for a funeral of an aged aunt she had never met. Apart from news she heard from her mother and father, her uncle and especially her grandfather, she knew little of the world outside her village. She knew how to tend hens; she knew how to kill and skin a goat; she knew how to cook ugali and rice and beans and every other dish she'd ever eaten since she was old enough to walk. She knew what was expected from her by her family and her husband. In an ancient ritual – more like a great party which every woman in the village danced and strutted – she had been shown how to wash, how to dress and move, how to please a man and how to give birth. Anna, her small wiry mother, with eyes like a small rodent, had reminded her often that to marry and have healthy children was the path to happiness and heaven.

Chapter Two

The bus-stand, an hour before dawn, was alive with men shouting through the thick exhaust fumes and the smoky fires cooking small white cobs of maize. Coach drivers sat nonchalantly aloft in their great thrones, looking down on the growing throng while their 'boys' scampered and heckled, loading bags into the filthy vaults under the coach and arguing with ticket touts over a spare seat here or a discount there. As the departure time of dawn approached, an audible tension grew, augmented in grades as coach after coach began revving their deep throaty engines, belching great clouds of black arid smoke.

It had been raining heavily for the several days; the bus station had been turned into a thick red slimy swamp in places where the great coaches had churned the wet ground. As the clock on the tower reached twelve thirty, - it was six o'clock in the morning, but the timepiece had never been mended - a whistle sounded from the corner of the bus station and the first bus thundered a reply with a loud revving of its engine. Slowly at first, then faster as more and more buses joined the great parade of beasts, they made their way out of the stand and on to the road. The buses edged their way round small wooden stalls selling bottles of pop and cigarettes and soap, past the young boys with great plastic buckets aloft, full of savoury bites or grilled calamari or greasy doughnuts. Finally, great blasts on their horns trumpeted their departure. The air filled with black smoke and dust as the great daily migration began.

All week the talk around town had been of strikes and violence, what local people would do to government officials if they interfered. For too long, the region had suffered neglect and discrimination by government. Too little had been done, there were few jobs, there was little investment and now Chinese and European investment was finally appearing, rumour had it that local people would gain nothing. There was a real sense of anger rippling around town. The District Commissioner had been on the radio calling for calm. Several mosques had inflamed matters the previous Friday by speaking of the need to stand up against injustice. Innocent's mother had asked if he could postpone his visit,

"There will be trouble on the road. What will happen if you can't get back?"

Innocent ignored her and continued to stuff his few belongings into a small scruffy rucksack.

There were more police than usual at the bus stand this morning. They strutted around, the sergeant clasping a short stick under his arm, occasionally wielding it to point to someone to move a motorbike or shift an old woman's things. On board the Sumy bus to Dar, Innocent sat nervously. He had made this trip only twice before – once with his mother when he was very young, which he remembered only in sounds and smells – the sounds of men shouting and the smells of deep fried chicken, both of which he'd experienced rarely before he was seven. The second time he'd been to Dar was last year when his uncle paid for him to visit him there. That had been the most exciting moment in his life. He would always remember the sense of wonder as he stepped off the bus in Dar. The sounds and smells this time were made intelligent as he looked around in wonder at the hellish chaos of traffic, street traders, and so many people standing, sitting, waiting. As he peered through the window in the dark, waving at young men he knew, hoping they would recognise him, he felt a boyish pride. One man looked, waved hesitantly but then put his arm back to his handcart and looked away. Innocent turned to the small TV suspended at the front of the bus and the loud garish *bongo fleva* videos that would play in a ceaseless loop for the next eight hours.

As the sky turned from deep dark blue to pale grey, the shapes of houses and fences appeared along the roadside. Men struggling on great iron bicycles loaded with great plastic sacks of charcoal, bundles of newly cut young trees, were making their way towards town. Women with great bundles or buckets atop their heads walked in single file, ignoring the warning blasts as the thundering coach sped past. At the first stop, where the bus lunged dangerously close to a waiting queue of travellers, there were the first signs of the unrest some had been talking about. A large man waving a *panga* was directing a motley

group of young men to carry large stones on to the road. Two others were hacking at a great flame tree as two others were dragging large branches from another tree to form a roadblock. Innocent's bus had already passed but he had to pray the trouble would be over before he returned. The driver was shouting something at the group of men out of the window. Innocent couldn't hear and he slid the window open. One of them looked up and smiled,
"Thanks brother. Have a safe journey."
The large man directing affairs looked less pleased.
"Don't drive today man. Join us. We have to show them that we won't stand for this treatment any longer."
"Good luck guys." And with that he placed his fist on his steering wheel and a great blast shook the small market. Women gathered their shawls, dragged their great bundles and babies and made their way down the bus. As the bus pulled away Innocent pressed his face against the window and saw some of the men throwing one or two items of rubbish at the bus. They had only sticks, not guns.

The journey gave Innocent no rest. The bus was crowded and noisy. A baby cried for almost forty minutes – his mother unable to satisfy him; an old woman with two hens and a toothless grin stopped the bus on the wild road miles from anywhere. She found the only empty seat, the row behind Innocent leaving her hen to scratch and shriek.

He slept for most of the journey but as the bus entered the outskirts of Dar, it joined a long line of traffic snaking its way into the city. The bus stopped and started, edging closer to the junction ahead where the bus station stood, a magnet drawing all within its range ever closer but moving ever slower.

As he stepped off the bus, swung his small bag over one shoulder, Innocent looked round for his uncle. He hadn't seen him for over a year and wondered if his appearance had changed. Once the hubbub around the bus had eased, families united, sacks of tomatoes unloaded, motorcycles called, he could see further. He looked over the waiting three-wheeler taxis and there, by the booking office, stood Thomas Mpanda, his uncle. He was wearing black laced polished shoes, bright purple trousers and a white shirt, smartly pressed. Perched on his head were large rimmed dark glasses, so he looked rather like a giant garishly coloured insect. He was tall and thin and greeted Innocent with a cursory passing of his palm across Samson's outstretched hand.
"How is it, boy?"

Thomas Mpanda was perhaps only five years older than Innocent but he seemed to possess the poise and confidence of someone infinitely wiser than the young nephew. More to the point, he loved showing it. He walked off gesturing to Innocent for him to follow behind. They walked three meters apart, Innocent skipping and tripping occasionally as he struggled to keep an eye out for Thomas and take in the marvels of this seething metropolis at the same time.

They walked for twenty minutes, through narrow streets of shacks and market stalls, past wooden houses and steel shuttered shops. They were walking through a maze of streets and alleys in the thronging market district in one of the many shanty suburbs of Dar. Formerly, an affluent area of low rise concrete shops and apartments owned by Asian traders, the area had become crowded with street stalls and hundreds of hawkers. Today, it is a sprawling labyrinth of shops, stalls, markets, cycle stands, traffic jams and baskets of fruit and vegetables. On a cement porch outside a small house, lay an old man, prone, with a small basket by his foot. One leg was thin and withered, the flesh pale and taught and the small foot turned in. He lay begging, using one hand to wave away flies and the other to scratch his sunken belly. Thomas greeted him,
"Hullo sir. How are you?"

The old man grunted a toothless reply and gawped at Innocent, shaking his empty basket. Thomas and Innocent stooped under the low doorway into a dark room at the far end of which was a small doorway leading to a yard where hens scratched and a small fire smoked between three blackened stones. Two women, wrapped in dark shawls sat hunched on the floor, one wafting the fire, the other sifting rice. Behind the women in the far corner of the yard, under a rough canopy made of straw and suspended by four wooden poles, sat three men sitting on a roughly made bench and an upturned bucket.

One of them, the youngest of the group, perhaps seventeen, wearing old white trainers and a black tracksuit, with a lion emblem of the chest, held a blue shoulder bag in front of him. He lifted from the bag two mobile phones and passed one to each of the other two men

"These are not so good, man. They are old."

"They will not sell even outside Dar. No-one wants these old phones."

The young man's face fell; he moved to take the phones from them

"I have others. And anyway, every phone sells. Everyone wants a new mobile."

As Thomas and Innocent made their way towards them the group turned,

"Good to see you. Did you have a good trip man?"

There was slapping of hands and between innocent and the youngest man a warm if awkward hug. They smiled and asked about each other's families. The older man in the group, who Innocent learned was called Elias, made to leave,

"Right now. I have some business to attend to. We'll meet at my store tonight. Now, you should eat something and sleep. Frank here will come for you later." He pointed to the young man with a twisted foot.

The men left and one of the old women showed Innocent to a low bed in a small dark room near the front of the house. He washed his hands and his feet under a tap and lay in the dank heat with the flies buzzing around him. For a moment or two he waved them away with his hand above his head but soon gave way to tiredness and closed his eyes. The noise of motorcycles, horns blaring and men shouting, at first, kept him from sleep but after only a few minutes his breathing grew deeper, his eyelids fluttered and his hand fell to his side.

He woke to the sound of a dog barking. At first, he thought the dog was in his room with him; he was disoriented; he took a moment to remember where he was. The dog was in the street immediately outside the small window above his head. Innocent knelt on the bed and pressed his face against the steel bars, peering left and right down the narrow street. It was dark and the noise of traffic on the main road seemed louder, the shouts of market traders having subsided. As he watched, one of the three men from earlier this afternoon, walked up the alleyway towards his room. He limped and dragged one foot behind him, leaving a trail of dust behind him. He called from outside the door and a voice from within greeted him. He stooped through the doorway. As he pulled his face from the bars, Innocent heard a voice behind him. An old woman was greeting him,
"Drink some sweet tea before you go out."
"No time for tea," called the young man, "Time to

move. Come with me Innocent, old man. We have to go to work."

An old flat back lorry was waiting on the main street. The older man from this afternoon was in the driver's seat; the other man was in the passenger seat. Innocent and Frank climbed into the back and sat on the wheel arches. They pulled away in a swirl of dust and bounced and bumped through narrow streets, furrows of caked mud made their passage slow as well as uncomfortable. After thirty minutes, they were in the heart of the city. Around them were buildings with glass fronts, traffic lights with long sleek cars and advertising boards lit with neon lights. Elias stopped at some lights and banged on the roof of the cab. Frank gestured to them to get out. Innocent followed.

They made their way to a small passage way next to a large warmly-lit restaurant selling Indian foods. Inside, on plastic chairs at small tables, sat a small number of Indian families. One group, close to the window where Innocent peered in sat a young fat boy in a deep purple *kameez*. He was eating a large bowl of curry. A young girl, his sister, was sipping at a bottle of coke through a straw. A woman, their mother, nibbled at a *pakora* with the tips of her fingers and dabbed her mouth every few seconds with a paper napkin. An older fatter man was reading and talking every now and then, over the top of his newspaper, to the fat boy opposite. A sleek expensive mobile telephone lay on the table in front of him.

Innocent and Frank sat back on their haunches. Frank took from his shirt pocket, a cigarette, one he had half smoked earlier. They sat in their own silence, Frank enjoying his cigarette and Innocent still bemused by the vastness of the buildings and the commotion around him. None of his childhood memories of his previous visit to Dar included such sights. His gaze followed passers-by, transfixed. When a new white Toyota cruised slowly past, Innocent's mouth opened and closed involuntarily. Frank sniggered and nudged him with a hoarse whisper,
"Innocent, old man. Shut it. You're catching flies."

The Indian family were moving; the man reaching into his large backside for his wallet; the woman ushering her children towards the door and smiling broadly at the owner. The fat boy was moving slowly, fingering the packets of sweets stacked on shelves near the door.
"Come on Akram. Quickly."

As they made their way along the covered walkway in front of the shops, Frank suddenly sprang to his feet. He waited until the fat old man was alongside the alley when he snatched from under his jumper, a short knife, the sort butchers used for paring slaughtered animals.
"Give me money. Now. And the phone. I want money. Now."

Innocent was transfixed. He was still sitting on his haunches.

"Give them to me now or I will slit your throat and he will take your daughter."
The mother grabbed the girl and ran.
"Innocent. Go. Take the boy."
The man started shaking. Frank held him by his throat and pressed him against the cement wall. The fat boy looked on crying. Innocent stood and grabbed the boy from behind.
"Give it to them daddy."
Innocent felt his arm relax from the young boy's throat. Sweat running down the base of his spine tickled as it reached his shorts. The boy's voice rasped; his hair smelt of soap and cooking oil. His chin felt bony and uncomfortable pressed against Innocent's arm.
"Here it is. But I have very little."
He held out his wallet. Frank held out his hand for the phone. The old man dropped it on the floor. Innocent bent to pick it up.
"Run Akram. Run!" The young boy ran across the street and disappeared between two market stalls, their plastic sheets flapping like lost sails hiding the boy's escape.

Frank watched for a moment then ran. Innocent looked for a moment longer then turned and ran. Innocent heard a man shout, "Stop." Frank was fast and Innocent soon lost sight of him, but he didn't stop. Innocent ran with his throat hurting. The fear and panic ripped into his chest; his breathing was fast and uneven. After some moments, he found another alley, unlit and dirty. He edged his way in the dark until he came to a small shrub, where he squatted and waited. His breathing sounded to him like a wounded animal and he clamped his mouth with his hand to try and stifle it. After a few minutes, his phone rang. He grabbed his pocket, trying to muffle the ringing and answer the phone at the same time.

"What?" Innocent's hand was shaking. "I don't know where I am." The voice from the phone became louder. Innocent's breathing eased slightly but his legs trembled.

After some time, before dawn, Innocent made his way from the alley back to the house in Kuriaku, where he had slept, going from landmark to landmark as well as he could. He could ask no-one because he knew no-one's name other than his uncle and the young thief who had just left him and because he was afraid that people might recognise him once the Indian family reported the crime. Eventually, as the sky once again turned to pale grey from deep indigo he came to the street he'd left yesterday evening. He recognised the small store selling sodas and bread, the wooden hand cart chained to the shop front and an old board, selling beer, with the words, "It's time to relax – it's Kili time."

****

The weeks passed. Innocent spent mornings around the house in Kuriaku, sipping sweet tea, chatting with the old women, occasionally dawdling to the shop at the end of the street where he could buy a cigarette or a razor. He had spent the few shillings he had in his pocket weeks ago and now relied on the tips and favours flung in his direction by Elias. Elias had called him a boy, a disappointment and a waste of breath. If he wanted to eat, he had to work and that meant the same work as Frank and the others. Innocent wanted most days to go back to his home, to Rose, to his mother, but he could ask no-one for the bus fare. He had thought of asking his mother or Rose but the disgrace of failure stopped him from sending the text.

After several days of sleeping, barely eating and slouching around the local area, he decided he had better make the best of it. He wouldn't risk stealing. Frank might steal but with a broken knife and a twisted foot, Innocent reckoned he would get caught and Innocent did not plan to get caught with him. But he could sell. His mother had always told him he had the gift of a silver tongue and now he could put it to use. He put it to Elias one morning when they came around to collect the previous night's booty,
"It's an idea. Try it. See how you get on."
Innocent had expected resistance, an argument, more abuse and ridicule. But no, Elias had agreed. Perhaps Uncle Thomas had more influence with Elias than it seemed. Families ran deep and memories were long.

Innocent would go that night towards the beach area where there were plenty of young people out for a night with money in their pockets.

Innocent had been selling since he could talk. As a boy he sold sweets, pencils, hens, spare parts for bicycles, old trainers, anything he could buy or trade. He never made much money but he had always had a few shillings in his pocket to buy a soda and impress the girls. Selling used, stolen phones to a sophisticated well-dressed customer in downtown upmarket Dar was a different matter. Perhaps it was his regional accent, perhaps it was his shy manner and cheeky swagger but young men as well as young women usually stopped to listen and each night he'd sell one or two – enough to impress Elias.

Frank came to stay in his house. They were very different – Frank was quiet but with a quick wit. He could read the local paper and together they would go through the football results. Usually on a Saturday afternoon they would wander down to a local bar where a small straw-roofed hut had been built with a large television on a rough shelf which stood high on one wall. This shack was crammed each Saturday afternoon with dozens of young men and for a few shillings every youth in the area could come to cheer on their team. Frank followed Chelsea whilst Innocent favoured Arsenal. But it mattered little. They shouted and jeered and laughed and whistled whoever was playing and slapped each other's shoulders as they walked home in the dark. At night Frank would take the bed and Innocent would make a mattress with an old blanket and using their clothes for a pillow and the following night, they would swap and Innocent would take the bed. Each morning Innocent would fetch water from a tap fifty yards down the street.

"You stay Frank. You take too long with your twisted foot." They would laugh. Frank would wait for his porridge in the yard and listen while the old women would cackle and gossip in their clucking whisper.

One night, after Innocent had sold two small phones to a couple of young women, he was showing a smart new Nokia to a young guy with shiny leather shoes and a fist full of gold, chains clinking and glistening on his wrist. One of the women came back to speak to Innocent.

"This phone is not so good, man. It switches itself off."

"Give me a minute girl. I'll show you." The young woman sighed and pouted and pointed one foot theatrically.

"Just give me my money back boy. This phone is no good."

Now the guy with the gold bracelets was interested,

"Let's see." He took the phone. "Yes. This phone is no good. Give her back her money."

Innocent could see a problem coming. He rammed his hands into his pockets and felt the roll of notes. He could give her the money or he could run. He needed the new Nokia back. Deftly he went to take the old phone off the old man, looking as if to inspect the goods before offering a refund, but swiftly, he snatched the new Nokia instead and ran. He guessed correctly that these three – dressed in dancing clothes as they were - would not give chase. Once clear of danger and hidden in the shadows of some huge lorries parked for the night, he phoned Frank. Frank's ansaphone cut in. Innocent sighed,

"Where are you? I've had some trouble. I'll meet you at the bus stand."

At the bus stand Innocent tried to wait in the shadows. The moon and the light spilling from the bar across the road lit the face of his phone, but made him feel naked and nervous. The bus stand was deserted but for an old man making a bed outside one of the coach booking offices. Two women were sitting on their haunches, tying plastic bags containing sweet cakes. They were laughing as they looked across at Innocent. He rolled under the rusty chassis of an old lorry, hidden from view by its wheels. From here he could watch the legs, the duty feet and the coloured skirts go by, unseen. He waited and watched. After a few minutes, his attention was drawn to three dogs fighting over a carcass. One of the dogs ripped it free and then hunched low over its prize, its teeth bared. A moment later, he shuffled and uncrossed his legs to watch two women talking. One was attending to the other's braids, weaving coloured cloth into the braid, whilst her client sat legs apart on the cool concrete verandah. Innocent squat in the shadows, under the old lorry, unseen.

It was getting late and some of the traders, the food stall and the hawkers of bracelets and dishcloths were packing their wares for the night. A group of men and women moved at speed into the bus stand. Innocent heard drums and whistles before he saw them. Some were shouting. A woman was heard wailing. Occasionally a glint of a reflection was seen waving in the air above their heads. They weren't running. Some were marching, younger boys were trotting or skipping. One man held a torch, a flaming rag tied to a stick. In front of the crowd a lone man walked, occasionally tripping and stumbling, his hands behind his back. As they moved nearer, Innocent could see from his vantage point on the raised walkway that the young man in the front of the crowd was Frank. His hands were tied behind his back and a rope from his wrists was being held by one of the men in the baying crowd. As they drew nearer, Innocent could see that many of them carried blades, large wide blades used by farmers.

At the bus stand the crowd moved faster and some ran around to encircle Frank; one approached him waving his blade; another threw a stone; another threw some mud. Suddenly a woman from the back of the crowd ran awkwardly and slashed at his shoulder with her blade. He tried to cover himself but his arms were tied and the blow caused him to fall. In falling, the crowd drew nearer and at once there were blades slashing and chopping. Innocent could hear nothing of Frank's cries over the jeers and shouts of the mob. One woman turned and the light caught her face. Blood was splattered across her mouth and as her chest heaved, she sighed her satisfaction as the blade swung loosely from her bloody hands.

Chapter Three

The muddy path wound from the village through some shrub-land, across a rickety wooden bridge over a murky stream. The occasional flame tree shaded the path for some sections where the grass was patchy and thin. Elsewhere on either side of the thin red path the grass was thick and green. Frogs squealed from a nearby pond and in the distance, could be heard the tinny throat of a distant motorbike. Two young boys were playing in the stream. They were naked and their dark skin was covered with pale streaks of russet mud. Their skin shone through in dark wet patches. As the two women walked slowly, carefully, across the makeshift bridge, they stopped playing.

"Good morning," said one, in the traditional respectful terms reserved for elders.
"Maharaba," said Rose, equally respectful of this important tradition. "Is this bridge safe?"
"Well it's slippy, but the wood won't break."

Rose and Janet made their barefoot way edgily across the thin wet beams. They were dressed in old, richly coloured kangas. They each scooped theirs up between their legs as they crossed the bridge. With the bridge behind them, they faced a long slow climb up the winding path to the big road and the clinic. They trudged one behind the other in silence. Neither woman slipped nor sighed.

Only when they reached the first turn in the path, some two hundred yards up the hill from the stream, did they stop, breathe deeply and turn to look round. Behind them the village looked small and tidy. The houses, straw-roofed boxes made of mud and sticks, sat neatly in a reddish clearing. The bustling town of Mbulu lay out of sight, over this next hill and their tiny village – a curious oversight of history – sat as it had for hundreds of years, untouched by the passing of time. The church of St Benedict built on open land outside town brought the village closer to town.

Rose did not realise how little she's thought or talked about sex until she became pregnant. Her friend Janet sometimes asked if she should have sex with boys when they asked and invariably Rose counselled against it. But she did not give much thought to whether she would now want to have sex with Innocent again, or indeed what future, if any, lay ahead with Innocent as the father of her child. Her child, unborn, was very real for Rose but as for the three times that she had had intercourse with Innocent, that seemed a lifetime ago.

Tall coconut trees towered over the place, shrinking the tiny hamlet. Beyond the village stretched maize fields and cassava. In the distance, the land disappeared into a haze of cloudy grey and white and far away the thin dark blue line of the ocean marked the horizon. As the path climbed steeply, great gashes of red earth bared themselves where torrents of rainwater had washed away the path. Here the two girls clawed up the bank, off the track and through the bush until the path appeared once again. At the road, they rested again. They sat, squat under a large flame tree and wiped their hands and their brows.

"How is the baby?" Janet nodded her eyes towards Rose's swollen belly.

"He's fine. It's me that's sweating."

After a few moments of silence, but for the shriek of cicadas, a pick-up could be heard struggling up the track. Even after the rain, the track was dusty in parts as the water ran off into the ditch so quickly and behind the truck a great brown cloud of dust chased it up the hill. The two girls shouted the driver and waved as they smiled. The truck came to a stop, and an old man with a black face, a shadow of grey hair and a toothless grin, smiled back.

"Get in. You'll make an old man very happy."

The two girls sprang to life and ran around to the passenger door.

"There's no room for two Baba. We'll both hop in the back." And with one long leg Janet was astride the truck offering an arm to Rose.

"I'll get in the front Janet," she said. "I don't much feel like a bumpy ride with this one."

Rose leaned herself into the passenger seat and the truck heaved itself up the hill, the old man leaning forward and peering under the rim of the steering wheel.

The truck was used for making the short ride to town. Mr Bakari owned a small piece of land in the hills above Mbulu. He farmed maize, cassava and some legumes. Often the little he took from the land did not even pay for the diesel, but the truck had been with him for so many years and it was worth so little, what his wife didn't know wouldn't hurt her.

"Why are you so late, Baba?" asked Rose. "It will be too warm to work when you get there."

"Oh, I just had some business to deal with in town. How is your mother? And the family?"

"We are fine. I'll be happy in a few weeks though."

They both looked down at her swollen belly. Mr Bakari nodded and chewed the small stick between his teeth. The whole village knew what had happened and where Innocent was now. And Rose knew what thoughts and gossip lay smugly behind that kind face. Innocent had run away, leaving the shame with his family. Rose had been reluctant at first even to admit it but the village knew everything soon enough. Innocent's mother had struggled for many years and to many this latest weakness came as no surprise.

But Rose also knew Mr Bakari. She'd heard the cries from his house when he beat his wife. She'd seen his wife, Magret, the morning after those nights, bleary eyed from tears and stiff from hidden bruises. And as she wondered about who he might tell, Rose saw clearly the huddle of old men, squatting and sitting in the shade of the mango tree. Each man had his own secret – not really a secret as their bullying was not hidden. They were just not discussed. A man's business was his own. If he needed money or, even better, came into some money, then that would be discussed; but which of them had to beat his wife to 'correct her behaviour' and which of them looked elsewhere, at night, for sex, that was no-one else's business.

Once the small truck, rounded the top of the hill, the clinic and the large white church came into view. Mr Bakari's truck had saved them a long walk on a dusty path under a hot sun. She should be grateful. But she wasn't. She wished she'd squat in the back with Janet. It would have been uncomfortable. It might even have been bad for her baby. But they would laugh and tease the boys as they sped past them on the road approaching the clinic. Two young girls enjoying life. Two young girls with their lives ahead of them. What would happen now? Would she go to school? Or would she take a job as a house-girl for an old man like Bakari? She shifted in the plastic seat. It was hot and her back was sticky with sweat. She ached and was tired all the time. Even the short walk up the hill from the village – a distance she would run normally – had tired her out.

She seemed to find herself nowadays planning for tomorrow but her plans for next year seemed like a fantasy. She could think about what she would eat tomorrow but had no idea about her life ahead. She could remember clearly how sharp and quick she would be in finishing her schoolwork, or in arguing with her friends or even in answering her grandfather in his long tortuous arguments; but, nowadays, her whole body, starting with her brain, seemed to have turned to a sweet sludge.

The truck came to an abrupt stop in front of a newish cement building with a shiny tin roof. Its walls were painted a garish pale blue. Cement steps rose to a broad veranda in front, sheltered by the overhanging roof. Under this canopy were some wooden benches on which sat a mixture of young and old people – predominantly young. Janet sprang first from the back of the truck and yanked open the passenger door.

"Come on, you elephant. Let's see what doctor has to say."

They climbed the steps, greeted old Mama Mbinga. She'd had fourteen children and only three had seen their fifth birthday. Only those that survived had anniversaries.

"Good morning Mama Mbinga. How are you today?"

"Fine girls. And you, young Rose. It must be nearly time. Who will be with you? Not her?"

Janet was hurt and showed it.

"Yes. Her. Janet. And my mother." Mama Mbinga nodded her head. Rose's mother was notoriously unreliable and it had been for that reason that she had asked Janet to be with her when the time came for the baby to be born. You had to write someone's name down on the form and Janet loved to see her name printed boldly on the official form from the Ministry.

They squished up on the bench and waited for her name to be called. Rose immediately took out her phone and like a scab that needs picking, she pressed a button to check for messages. Nothing.

"Looking at it every minute won't make him remember you. You know that, don't you?"

Janet envied Rose. She envied her, her coppery complexion, her wiry figure and her quick wit. She had envied Rose since first they became friends chasing each other outside church. At one time, she would have envied Rose for her boyfriend more than anything. Seeing her now, she wasn't so sure.

Somewhere in the room an SMS message received rang out. She glanced down, pressed the buttons and held her head to one side in resignation. Nothing. How had she got to this point? Waiting, only waiting for a young man; wishing her life away; ignoring her senses and believing that Innocent would one morning become a different person.

"You can go in now," Mama Mbinga directed them to the closed door at the end of the hall. Rose knocked gently and half opened the door.
"Come in. Come in please," a sharp confident voice

rang out. Dr Gertrude was a tall, slim European woman with blond hair that she wore with a fringe and which she regularly flicked behind her ear. She had worked in this clinic for the past twelve months and had replaced an older African man who few trusted.

Dr Gertrude was seemingly always happy, as she smiled permanently. When she had first arrived at the clinic, older women sucked their teeth in disapproval. She wore skirts which showed her knees; she spoke hardly any of their language other than the most basic greetings and she had a peculiar smell. In fact, as the months passed and her treatments, especially for infections, seemed to work so well and so quickly, she gained the trust of the villagers. Rose preferred to come to this clinic rather than the big hospital in town simply because of Dr Gertrude.

The doctor examined Rose and asked her some simple questions about how she planned the delivery, explained what foods she should try and eat and encouraged her to return to the clinic regularly as the due date approached. Rose listened carefully but her mind wandered to the luxury of being spoken to so attentively and heard the warm sounds rather than absorbed the content of what Dr Gertrude was saying.

As Rose tied her kanga again, Janet asked,
"Do you think, doctor, that we could be nurses in this clinic?"

"There's no reason if you study hard that you shouldn't both become doctors or nurses. Which do you prefer?"

Both girls laughed and without answering, thanked the doctor and left.

As they walked home Janet asked Rose if there was any news from Innocent. He had sent SMS messages. How did she feel? At first, she was angry and excited equally. The blood rushed so that she could feel every nerve in her face and her hands became sweaty.

"I want you to come to Dar and live with me there," he asked. No introduction. No explanation. She called the number.

"And where would we live? Have you found work?" She knew the answer before she asked.

"We could..," he started with a stammer.

"No. Innocent. We could not. If you want to be with me you must come back to Mbulu and marry me here." Rose had hoped not so long ago that her wedding would be a joyful occasion full of romantic plans and tables of roses – 'a rose for my Rose', her grandfather would say.

"There's nothing for me there, Rose. I feel there are more chances in Dar. Won't you come and see?" He was pleading. She wanted to hold him, to touch him at least, but her reason was stronger than her instincts and she stood firm.

"Innocent. You should know that I want to be with you but I can't be with you unless we live a life where we can both feel good about what we do. What would

I do in Dar with a baby where I know no-one? Come to your senses, please."

He ended the call.

That had been after two months. Since then she'd heard nothing.

Chapter Four

For the seventh or eighth time that night, an old man nearby, coughed and coughed until he retched. A woman's voice nearby, too quiet to understand, scolded him back to sleep. Innocent turned. And turned again. He was hot and when he was awake he was hungry. Always hungry. And thirsty. At least the old man had a roof and a cot. For the second night Innocent had made his bed under the great shadow of a rusting lorry, its thick black wheels providing shade and the gloomy frame of steel and wood, stained with oil and diesel, offering him stinking shelter from the rain, should it fall. It didn't rain. Had it rained, perhaps the air would be clearer; perhaps his throat less choked with dust; his clothes, his eyes, his hair and his nose less clogged with fine brown dirt, driven by the swirling, morning breeze. He crawled out from under the lorry. It was still dark. The buses leaving the bus stand were revving their engines boasting plumes of black exhaust. Innocent had to find someone to take him. He couldn't stay in this town a day longer.

Each bus he asked, the answer was the same,
"You know, man, if it was up to me, I'd say yes. But the boss won't allow it and I'll be for the chop if I let you and he finds out. I can't take the risk." They didn't all say as much as this one but it amounted to the same thing. He made his way across to the docks. There, there were lorries, waiting to be loaded with

containers. He could beg a lift perhaps. He'd make a good guard. But it wasn't so simple.

"What do you mean? You can't ride outside. Only in the cab, and I already have someone." Lorry after lorry, one after another, the response was the same. One wizened old man told him to try his luck at the other gate. He trudged up the road, the emptiness in his stomach spread to his head with a dull ache. By midday, he had taken to walking slowly past each cab, showing his thumb in vain hope. Drivers shook their heads, looked the other way, stared past him, continued their idle talk. He came to a group of men squatting round a small fire. One man was turning cobs of maize on a tray, a sweet burnt smell in the air. He greeted them and waited. One of the group looked up and greeted him. After what seemed a long time, he invited Innocent,

"Karibu." Innocent moved a step closer and squat on the edge of the circle. They were drivers waiting for their containers to be cleared. He could not understand a lot of what they said – strange terms, references to places and people he did not know, abbreviations he had never heard. No matter, they were drivers, they had a fire, they had food, they were company and they did not seem like they were going to harm him. He rocked ever so slightly on his haunches. The conversation turned to troubles at the border.

"Immigrants."

"Not immigrants. Refugees."

"Same thing. They come here with nothing. With only

robbery in their minds and badness in their hearts."

"One boy was turned back with no papers. I saw them slap him. They hurt him. And cut him."

"It's true. However hard you think your life is, you wouldn't want to be them."

The talk of foreigners seemed to be the cue for one of them to turn again to Innocent.

"Where are you from boy? Where are you going? I've seen you walking this line looking for a ride."

"I'm heading south." He looked around the group with what he gauged was a hopeful grin.

"You running from something, boy?" asked one. Innocent stayed dumb.

"How much can you pay?" asked another.

"He's got nothing," said a third. "Look at him. Mudi, have you got room?"

A surly looking man with a scrawny beard and a grimy *kofia* looked up from the fire, giving Innocent the once-over, before returning his stare to the embers.

"Maybe." Innocent rocked on his haunches again.

As it happened, Mudi needed someone to help him. He had a twisted leg and could not secure the tarpaulin on his wagon well without help. He needed help climbing up on the truck and he had no strength to tie the ropes tightly. He gestured to Innocent with a nod only, what he should do and grunted when he'd done the job to his satisfaction. Innocent, for the first time in a long time, felt good about himself, doing this simple work. It had been a long time since he'd done something strenuous, helpful and honest. They left before the sun rose, as the sky was turning a dull grey and before the ugliness of the city became too stark.

The streets were empty at first, but as the sun quickly rose so the roads clogged with bicycles, small buses and motorbikes. When he sat high up in the cab alongside Mudi, he couldn't stop smiling and waving at young boys as Mudi swung the great wagon round tight corners, down narrow streets, abreast small shops and stalls, leaving a trail of thick dust behind. After perhaps an hour, Innocent stopped smiling and instead affected that studied nonchalant look copied from Mudi, of a man who'd been here all his life and had seen all life had to offer. Inside, his excitement made his skin prickle. The lorry was carrying a mixed load for an Asian trader by the name of Sumry. They were carrying plaster, cement, plumbing parts and fittings and about fifty mattresses. The lorry was an ancient British lorry with a great shuddering gear lever and which Mudi showed great skill in waving to select the gears. The cab was dirty, its floor littered with plastic bottles and newspaper. A string of brown prayer beads swung from a mirror in the centre of the cab.

Mudi spoke little. He asked few questions and Innocent felt strangely nervous to ask him anything. Once they had left the madness of Dar, Innocent's mind turned to his arrival home. He aimed to drop off at Lindi and make his way west to his village.

Eventually, as the sun rose higher and the traffic thinned, he slept, his head slumped into his chest and swaying viciously each time Mudi braked hard for a small stopping bus or a policeman stationed ahead. The lorry was old and progress was slow. Around two o'clock they stopped and Mudi fell asleep almost immediately. They started again an hour or so later, but the wagon seemed to be making even slower progress and trailed at walking pace up some of the inclines.

Innocent slept again but it was late afternoon when he woke as Mudi was climbing down from the cab. They had pulled over on a straight stretch of road in some open country, bush and small trees and in the distance some small grass-roofed houses. Innocent climbed down also and peered under the trailer to watch Mudi examining the underside of the cab. Black oil dripped steadily from somewhere to the rear of the cabin.

"Cut down some branches and throw them in the road." Mudi jumped back up to the cabin to drag down a square tin with some old tools.

Innocent knew what to do. Buses and lorries broke down all the time and this simple warning in the road to oncoming drivers was a common scene. He took the *panga* from behind Mudi's seat and began to traipse back down the road looking for a good-sized tree from which to cut the branches. He had to walk some hundred yards or more to find a good tree but he started to work immediately to hack at some of the longer branches. He left one in the road where he cut it and dragged two more with him to leave in the road at intervals between the tree and the wagon.

A small pick-up overtook him as he laid the second branch, swerving close to Mudi's wagon and stopping suddenly with a puff of dust and the sound of tyres skidding. Innocent watched, at first transfixed, then he moved to run towards them, then stopped again. From the back of the white pick-up leapt three men. Two immediately climbed up to the trailer while the third approached Mudi. Innocent could only just make out Mudi's shape in the failing light and couldn't hear anything said. Mudi was waving his arms as the man raised a stick and beat Mudi over the head. Mudi bent double then fell to the ground with a second blow and the man swung the stick again, bashing the end of the stick into Mudi's chest and face. Innocent slipped into the bushes at the side of the road and watched for what seemed a long, long time as the three men now dragged boxes from the trailer and lifted them into the back of their pick-up. Innocent lay still, eyes staring, listening intently as the pick-up drove away. Dirt had stuck to the sweat on the back of his neck which smeared as he wiped it. A stubborn droplet made its way from his hairline down the side of his cheek and nestled in the pool below his collar bone. He watched his T shirt move up and down in time to his hoarse breathing, and he saw himself standing up and running towards the thugs, shouting and waving and the thugs running, startled.

Innocent saw this clearly as he lay and watched his chest heave to the rhythm of his breath. The young man running bravely at the thugs looked back at Innocent hiding in the shrub.

"What would Jesus do?" sneered his grandmother. She was long dead but he remembered clearly her bony finger, her taunts jabbing his chest. As a young boy, his older sister, Teresia, had protected him from the taunts and the slaps and the beatings from his grandmother. Teresia had often looked on as Innocent was whipped or slapped for spilling water or failing to sweep the yard outside their small mud home. He remembered well as he lay in the shrubs and Mudi lay in a heap by the great wheel of his truck.

Perhaps ten minutes elapsed before another lorry trundled past up the hill. It stopped alongside Mudi's truck and two men got out, their engine still running. They helped Mudi to his feet and dragged him to the edge of the road, propped his limp body against one of the great black tyres and leaned over him to talk. One of them passed him a bottle, perhaps water. It was dark now and Innocent carefully walked away, using the shadow of the bushes to hide his flight.

Chapter Five

The baby was born at the hands of Rose's mother and an old neighbour who had brought medicine with her and a small bandage to tie to the baby's wrist to ward off evil spirits. In the end, despite the encouragement of the white doctor, she'd had the baby at home. When her contractions started, she decided that it was too far to risk the long walk up the hill to the new clinic. She managed on her own, only calling out for her mother at the very end. Her mother came running with a knife and cut the baby's cord and took the baby away to wrap it in a clean sheet and an old blanket. Rose lay alone in the dark. Cold and damp; one moment a stabbing pain, the next, shivers; even though she cried, she felt happier than she could ever remember. Mtandi – the old woman – held her hand and muttered old sayings in her old tribal language. Rose had focused on the pain – like her mother had told her – pushed hard when her mother told her and lay still when her mother told her. Now it was over. She felt spent, limp, empty and so very, very happy.

After some little while, her mother returned.
"Where's the baby, mama?"
"It's ok. But it's better if it's kept warm. I've wrapped him. And soon I will bring him to you."

Rose wanted to hold the baby. She had not thought that a baby would mean so much. She had held babies, washed them, cleaned them and fed them since she could remember. She did not give them much thought. Unless they were ill or did something very bad, they did not feature in her life. But now, suddenly, this baby meant so much. She'd carried it, felt it move, suffered swollen ankles and so much pain. Now she was angrily impatient to see it, to touch it, to hold it.

"Is old mother Mtandi holding him? Please tell her. I don't want him to have her medicine."
"What do you mean? She knows what's good for him. He seems weak. She will just prepare some herbs to give him strength and keep away evil. The devil takes them when they are weak like this."

Rose struggled to heave herself from the low cot in which she was prone. Her abdomen was hurting and as she twisted, a sharp pain made her yelp.
"No! I don't want it. Tell her no." She couldn't remember ever speaking to her mother so harshly. Her mother clicked her tongue and looked down at her.
"Who are you to speak like that? Mama Mtandi is here to help. Show some respect."

But Rose knew that her mother had understood. Even though she had admonished her, her mother was neither strong-willed enough nor held such harshness towards her daughter not to respond. She sighed and left her again, but this time Rose heard voices in the next house, muffled by the chirrup of cicadas and the thick warm night air. After a few more minutes as Rose lay, her mind roaming from the sensations of stinging pain, to deep tiredness then straining to understand the muffled voices and then listening to dogs barking and the screech of a faraway bird, she kept returning to the thought of her own small baby wrapped in her mother's kanga, waiting to be fed.

"Here he is." Her mother pushed the door expertly with her shoulder and passed the small bundle to Rose. She used her fingers delicately to peel away the cloth from around his face and hold the tiny head to her face, then to her breast. She rubbed her nipple up and down the tiny lips and felt the small pain in her breast and her belly as his toothless gums gripped.

The days passed quickly. People came and went, Rose prepared food, she slept, fed her baby and more people came. Her grandfather came to visit and peered into the baby's face. He looked at the baby boy for a long, long time, then clicked his tongue, stroked the baby's cheek and stooped low out of the house. He didn't say a word to Rose but she smiled. She knew her grandfather quite well.

Once the soreness had eased Rose began to feel happy with life with her new baby. The fuzziness in her brain and the aches and stiffness were quickly distant memories and she started to take intense, pleasure from unfolding and folding the few baby clothes she and her mother had managed to collect. She kept them in a small plastic bag on the one cupboard they possessed. Her mother had given her a plastic bowl in which to wash the baby. She started to build a simple routine in her mind – waking, feeding, washing, sleeping, feeding. The baby woke often and there were few hours in a day when Rose could sleep without interruption. She loved the early morning, before the sun had risen, when the air was cooler and the baby slept. She made her plans, for clothes, for her boy to go to school, for her own house and for brothers and sisters. The young girl in the white coat was somewhere in the distance. Now her dreams were for her family. Her grandfather came around again that evening.

"So, my daughter, are you happy with your new life?"

"Very happy, thank you, granddad."

"Really? This is what you want? Like your mother? And what of him? What do you want for him?"

"Grandad. He is a baby. His little cord's still pink and wet. What have you got to say about his future?" The old man shook his head and Rose looked at her baby's face while she thought of the hours she spent listening to her grandfather's stories.

Only he –alone in the village – stood out with these ambitions. Only he – talked about in villages across this wide valley – took such an interest in his children, and a grand-daughter at that. His chums laughed gently when he sat with them in the shade of a great mango tree in the morning, but he listened and looked at his feet and kept his thoughts to himself.

His stories were stories that he had heard when he was a child; stories of old chiefs and long walks, brave men fighting lions and children being trampled by elephants; stories of women wailing when babies died, when the water turned black and more babies died; when the village caught antelope and the whole village danced for a week; when his brother coughed, became sick and died in a day.

After a week, the baby's cries were weaker yet harsher. Rose fed him but he wouldn't suck and instead drew his spindly legs to his stretched stomach, opened his toothless mouth and bawled.

"Mama, what shall we do? I can't risk taking him all the way to clinic."

Anna had that stoical look on her face, the one she had when the rains stopped early; the one she had the morning after Rose's father had left her - a brief affair which she didn't expect to last and was ready for the bitter disappointment.

"I'll fetch Mama Mtandi. It can't harm." This time Rose held her pained expression but said nothing, just stroked her baby's tight tummy.

After a few hours, the crying became weaker – more a whimper than a cry – and his legs limp and floppy. After a few more hours, the crying stopped and the baby's breathing became shorter; his tight little chest pumping in and out like a thin veil in a breeze.

Chapter Six

A new day dawned. Not a trumpeted dawn with piercing orange rays, but a slow faded wash through the sky, replacing the blue blackness of night with a warm dull grey blanket. Innocent sat huddled on the back seat of an old daladala creaking and bouncing its way from village to village, stopping at every dusty track along the way to collect or leave passengers with bags, hens, sugarcane – whatever. He had slept at the bus stand with some young boys.

Some of them had been smoking a local hash and at one point the night looked as though it might become violent, but they were in high spirits and did no more harm than smash a basket, left out by an old woman selling tomatoes. They'd kicked it around and played a game with plastic bottle tops and the basket as a target. Some of them took the game too seriously and arguments ensued, the basket was tipped over and the bottle tops scattered.

He hadn't really slept. He'd dozed, tried to be comfortable, propped up in the small shelter, back against the pool table, covered for the night with a plastic sheet. He was grateful when he started to hear the first movements from some of the houses nearby. Women were moving about, washing, going to their toilet, banging pans. It was still dark but he approached one house where a small shape was huddled over a large pan starting a small fire.

"Morning mama. How is it?" And the usual pleasantries ensued, with the woman adding for good measure,
"You slept out there? Did the dogs not bother you?"
Innocent forced a cheery, nonchalant tone.
"No. It was fine. For one night, at least." He waited and peered into the darkness, for all the world as though he were expecting an old friend to come bounding out of the shadows. The woman looked into the trees as well, then turned to him
"I'm making porridge. Will you have some?"
"Ah no. Thanks. I'm still full"
"Really. I have made a little too much"
"Ah well. Perhaps a small cupful. Thanks." And he sat down on his haunches, rocked a little and watched as three small children, waddled out of the house and sat next to their mother as she stirred the old pan.

After he'd eaten his porridge he waited outside the one store made from cement blocks. Here the storekeeper spent a long time lifting out buckets, pans, brooms for sweeping, sacks of maize flour and rice and some yellow bottles of oil. Innocent moved in quickly, lifting out the heavier items and arranging them the way he thought the old storekeeper would want them. He then asked the old man if his wife would need firewood and before he could answer Innocent had snatched the 'panga' and ran off into the trees. He returned an hour later with a good bundle of sticks tied with grass. He tipped the bundle down and waited. The old man was curious.

"Where are you from? And where are you going? You're not from round here."

"You are right. I will be moving on today." And he stood and waited. But the old man hadn't finished.

"So where are you headed?"

"Lindi. Near Lindi." And he waited. Eventually, the old man took a crumpled note from a roll in his pocket and peeled it off for Innocent.

Now, squashed up against the window of this old daladala, Innocent had time to think. His mind turned to things he didn't want to think about. Of course, he wondered what had happened to the driver, Mudi. They would pass that spot very soon and Innocent already knew that he no longer had faith to pray that he wouldn't be there. He wasn't sure he had what the priest called 'faith' anymore -or even if he had ever believed in God who saw everything, knew everything and yet seemed to do nothing. He knew that the truck would still be there; he expected a crowd of people staring and pointing at him as he sped past. "What was he supposed to have done?", he heard himself calling back at their sneering. He was one young man alone against three harsh men. No-one called, no-one jeered; but Innocent heard them all the same.

The daladala bounced and creaked on towards Lindi. He called out to the driver from the rear of the bus where he was squeezed in between two large women. The driver pulled over. Innocent couldn't even be certain of the precise route home but when they had reached a junction he thought he recognised he called the driver to stop, clambered over the bodies squashed into the van and jumped out. He began the long walk home. When he arrived at the broken walls of a primary school he knew exactly where to go. With such an early start, he should reach his village before nightfall. He soon left the main road and took a wide unmetalled road leading west. In the distance a great wooded escarpment, occasionally gashed with red clay, shone through the haze. He slipped into a loping stride which gave him a good pace and which made him feel good. He had done little exercise in his time in Dar and for once it felt clean to be outdoors, stretching and moving. There was a slight breeze which only served to perfect the moment. He wondered why events conspired to give him such trouble. Only at moments like this could he ever admit even to himself that he was a coward and a cheat.

As he walked he tried to construct a story of his life, told to himself in the manner of the elders he heard recounting oral histories. He couldn't get much beyond a series of images in a virtual photo album, starting with him as a baby. There had never been a photo of course, but he had a 'memory' constructed for him by his mum of a small house and a baby in a bowl for a bath. As he turned the pages he wanted to see strong happy images of him smiling at school playing football, but the photo that intruded was the one of him furtively beating a young boy. He couldn't recall now why but he thought it was something to do with the need to show his friends. The young boy was badly beaten and had done nothing. He tried to see pictures of him copying his notes from school, but instead the big colour photo was of him stealing money from his mother. She asked everyone and Innocent even offered to fight the young boy he said he suspected. His mum stroked his head and said, 'No, son. They will get their just deserts.' Had he ever done anything good, anything of which his mother could be proud? He'd even left Rose. He'd said he'd call but he never did. He put in place the photo of him and his father; but it slipped and was soon replaced by a torn picture of him selling cigarettes near the bus stand. He remembered for no apparent reason his first Communion. Here was something he could keep hold of. Here was something in which he believed, something to give him some pride. But then he thought of his days in Dar, the bad things he'd done and the times he could have prayed and didn't. He was climbing now and his reflections were pushed aside as he took care to climb and keep up a good pace.

He would cut across country soon, finding those faint tracks he had used as a boy. He tried to resolve to be different but before he could plan his thoughts around seeing Rose, cultivating some land, going to church and living a good life, it was quickly replaced by the thoughts of when he might return to Dar and all those bad thoughts which undid him so easily. For now, he thought of his mum and hoped she would smile when she saw him.

"Hullo there. What's your news?" The greeting shook him from his reverie.
"Fine, Father. How are you? You look well."
"I'm alive and have food enough. Where have you been? You're old mother Jacob's boy, aren't you? Been away and up to no good I'll bet. Have you brought riches home to your mother? Have you many cows?"
Innocent laughed and said he'd not but that he'd come home to look after his mother. He'd been away too long and it was time things changed. The priest sighed and although he put his arm around Innocent's shoulder, he knew these were empty words.
"What's your name?"
"Innocent, Father."
"I'm Gerold Mkati. I've been a parish priest for over ten years, Innocent. And I think life is getting harder not easier. What have you learned while you've been away?"

Innocent looked down as they walked. The priest was barefoot and his trousers were rolled up to his knees. He was carrying a hoe over his shoulder and a sack that was empty but for a small bulge that moved as it draped over his back.
"In Dar, I'd be driven around town in a shiny clean car. I'd live in a house with water and sheets. And I'd

have a man to cook for me and empty the latrine."

Innocent said nothing. He was still thinking about what he'd learned. He watched a line of women in the distance picking their way through the fields carrying buckets and hoes on their heads.

"I must have done something very wrong for the bishop to leave me here without even a motorcycle. How does he think I can say Mass and baptise babies in three churches when all I have is a broken bicycle? He must be very angry with me. Did you know that Father Fortunatus has a Landrover? For one month's plate collections, he could fix the brakes and it would be safe to drive."

Innocent listened at first but as the old priest droned, Innocent's thoughts wandered. Why could he not be satisfied? Why did he find it so hard to make the right decision? Why so often did he know the right thing to do and then just as soon as the idea of fast money, easy girls or new clothes popped in his head, Pop! Out goes his fine decision. Why did some boys – boys he'd grown up with – find it so much easier to stay in their village, respect their fathers and even dig the land? They seemed happier, more content with their lives. He'd need a father, first, before he could respect him. That's a point.

"And as for me," droned Father Gerold, "I must live on porridge and beans. I must dig my own garden. If I have hens, I must kill them myself. This is not how a priest should live. I bring Christ into people's lives – with these worn old hands – the same hands that must plant maize brings Christ to life through the bread of the sacred host. This is God's will – certainly the bishop's – but I will never understand it."

Innocent did not truly understand. He had believed in the powerful magic of the Mass, but it troubled him to hear the priest speak like this.
"The bishop's newsletter arrived in the post last week and told of important meetings in Dar. Every priest in the country should have been there. Thousands of goats had been killed to feed everyone. Me – I haven't enough for a bus ticket."

Innocent felt uncomfortable listening to the priest's intimate complaints. These things were best kept private.

They walked together – the old man and young Innocent – their strides equal but their thoughts very separate. Occasionally, one would point out the skin of a dead snake or a trail of biting insects. The other would peer far away for signs of life in the village at the foot of the distant hill, thin trails of smoke blurring an otherwise stark blue sky. The first sight of the village was through the branches of the flame trees after the brow of the hill. The two men lengthened their stride as they headed downhill. Some children stopped playing as they went past, one or two older ones went to touch Fr Gerold's hand as he passed. They looked suspiciously at his companion. Innocent surprised himself at the disappointment he felt at not being recognised or remembered. How could they? These children were too young. And yet, still, it stung a little. As they approached the church, Gerold stopped to shake Innocent's hand,

"Have you a drink of water at your house, Father?"
"Yes. I have. And so has your mother. Do you not want to greet her?"
"I will do soon. I would prefer to wash my hands and face before I see her. Do you mind?"
"You are a strange boy. Yes. Come with me."

Together they crossed the open land in front of the only brick building for miles around; a wide European design with thin windows and a green copper ribbed roof. It had water pipes and glass windows. It had a great wooden door atop stone steps. Inside, it had electric strip lights and dozens of wooden pews. Behind the altar, stretched the wracked body of Christ against a hewn cross made of local wood. In a corner, in front of a small plaster statue of the Virgin Mary, sat three plastic chairs. An old woman was on her knees washing the floor.

Gerold led the way round to the rear of the church and a single storey building of blocks with a corrugated iron roof and windows covered with metal bars and iron mesh. Gerold left his bags on the small concrete veranda, unlocked the door, removed his shoes and made his way into a large room and heaved himself into a great sofa of red velveteen with heavy wooden arms. A dining table covered with a plastic cloth sat in the middle of the room. In the centre of the table stood a crucifix of black wood. Innocent sat briefly in a plastic chair by the table then stood suddenly and asked if he could wash himself,

"Through there," pointing towards a curtain hiding the doorway through to a small room with a sink and a tall painted cupboard. Below the sink sat a plastic bowl with a plastic pouring jug. Innocent washed his head and his hands and found a cloth hanging from the side of the sink with which to dry himself. When he returned to the larger room, he found Gerold already asleep.

"I'll go Father," Innocent shook the old man's shoulder gently.

"Yes." He stirred and rubbed his head. "You go. And greet your mother. Tell her that I have returned her prodigal son. Tell her to kill that fatted calf." He laughed so loudly at his own joke that he started coughing and spluttering. Innocent used this opportunity to smile and leave.

He crossed the village to a huddle of small houses of mud and thatch. The red earth around each of these houses was pounded flat and smooth. When it rained, no grass or weeds could stem the water and the space quickly became a stream that left grooves and small valleys in the red earth. Outside one small house sat a woman of perhaps forty – but she could easily be thirty or fifty – squat on a tiny wooden stool. She was working maize with a pestle and next to her a fire struggled to burn amid three round stones.

A small child of perhaps two years, naked except for a torn t-shirt, played aimlessly with a stick making shapes in a patch of mud, made wet from the old woman's work. The woman looked up at Innocent has he passed. He greeted her and the old woman responded mechanically without breaking the rhythm of her pounding. Innocent made his way through the houses to one with a broken roof and no door. Some pieces of kanga had been hung in the doorway. Innocent rapped on the door frame,
"Hello. I am here." Nothing.
"Hello," Innocent called the traditional polite greeting for entering someone's home.
"Karibu. Welcome." A faint voice came from the darkness behind the cloth doorway.

Innocent stooped to move into the dark inner. He stood for a moment to allow his eyes to adjust to the darkness and lit by light from one small opening in the far wall and some sharp rays piercing the thatched roof lay his mother, on some matting, propped on one elbow.
"Mother. It's me. Innocent. Are you well?"
"Innocent? Is it really you? Come here so I can see you better."

He bent down for her to peer into his face. She stretched out her hand to hold his face, then smartly snatched it away. Some flies had been attracted to his mother's head and she waved them away.

"So. You've returned? Are you in trouble?"

"No. I've come home because I wanted to be with my own people. Perhaps it was a mistake."

Innocent had thought this line of explanation would invite few awkward questions. It left the questioner proud of their provenance and with perhaps a slightly higher opinion of the respondent than they would otherwise have.

"Go and see old man Gugu to tell him you've returned. He will make a small offering for me."

"Later, mum. It can wait. First I must eat and you must tell me all the news of the village."

"If it's food you want, you will have to go to Mama Shafi. She will have porridge. Tell her I sent you."

With that she closed her eyes and lay back down on her mat. She waved weakly again at the flies. Innocent first looked, waited, then backed out of the room into the bright sunshine.

He made his way back to the church where he found Gerold, now awake and filling buckets of water from the tank to the rear of the church.

"Ah. Good. You can help me carry this water inside. I must shower after my long walk. Thank God it has rained here and my water tanks are full."

Innocent said nothing, but carried the bucket of water inside. He refilled it and repeated the task several times until the large plastic bin in the back of Gerold's dark house was full.

"She was not pleased to see you?" Innocent did not know how Gerold knew of his mother's reaction. "You must eat with me. You can start by preparing the beans. I have brought a scrawny hen with me today. You can kill it and tonight we will have our own feast. You will find some spinach in the small garden through there." He pointed to a small patch of cultivated earth where some pale green spinach grew and the remains of some maize plants stood stark and bare.

As he prepared the meal later that afternoon, he reflected on his mother's reaction. Should he feel angry? Hardly. He had been away for many months, had never sent her money nor enquired of her health. He realised as he worked that he was grateful to the priest. He was grateful for the chance to do something. Innocent thought he felt something like satisfaction. He had been spurned by his mother, he had fled the scene of a horrible crime with shameful cowardice and he had not had the courage to greet the mother of his yet unseen child. And yet, picking and washing spinach, lighting a fire, killing and plucking a hen and boiling beans for the priest's supper gave him the first fleeting sensation of doing something worthwhile – something from which he stood to gain nothing other than a meal and for which the priest may or may not be grateful. But for the first time that he could remember Innocent felt useful, wholesome, almost whole.

As they ate their supper, Gerold spoke again of Innocent's mother.

"My difficulty is Innocent that as a Catholic priest I offer salvation to everyone. They must have their children baptised; they must bring them to church, learn their catechisms and confess their sins. If they believe in God and the Church they will be saved and when they die they will go to heaven. Your mother, like many women in the village, is happy to do all that. I have no difficulty in finding women to clean and scrub the church each week. They beat their children if they do not stay quiet in church and they bring me gifts each Sunday. But they will do the same for the witch doctor and they will pray with the Muslims as well when they are asked. As a boy, I'm sure your mother had you wear the small coloured bracelet to ward off evil spirits. She certainly asked me to bless the house. Only last week I was asked to perform an exorcism. All the children had fallen ill and their milk cow had died. They were convinced that evil spirits were to blame and that an exorcism would put things right. I didn't need to do that. The bishop disapproves of that sort of thing happening too often nowadays; but I re-blessed the palms they had received on Palm Sunday, urged them to place one above each doorway and say the Rosary together each evening before supper. They were so happy they paid me with a huge stick of bananas."

The next day, Innocent went again to his mother's

house and followed her to the field where she worked and without comment, worked all day by her side. He dug the soil, removed weeds and fetched water to where the plants needed it. It was hard work, but like yesterday with Gerold, it was work that left him feeling somewhat complete.

His mother was softening, too. She felt his face as he slept and felt happy again. She thanked God for his return and burned juju herbs as thanksgiving.

Chapter Seven

Babu Jackson buried the baby with care but without ceremony. He'd done it several times before. Rose stayed inside. She'd wailed for almost an hour but now she felt numb, empty. Her mother had taken the baby clothes away and now there was no trace that a baby had ever been there. Babu Jackson did the grim task alone. He'd told no-one, used his old hoe to dig a good hole and said his own prayers while he was digging. He dug it deep and placed three large stones on the fresh earth to mark the spot and in the hope that animals didn't disturb it. He came back to Anna's house to tell them where the baby was buried.

"God decided to take that baby away. Now you can return to school."

Even her mother was shocked at her father's brutal approach.

"I can't believe you're saying that Babu. And I'll decide what I want to do with my life."

"Ha! Listen to her. 'I'll decide.' You'll decide nothing. When you've got shillings of your own then maybe you can start deciding things. Til then show some respect." Silence. Rose had acquired a new resilience and was not to be bullied. Anna, so often the victim, stepped in.

"Stop it the two of you. This is not the right time for shouting and fighting."

Rarely did Anna interfere in the close sometimes hostile relationship between Jackson and his granddaughter, but she was grieving too. She had buried too many babies and it never got easier. This latest death brought back for Anna the babies of her own who had died, those of her sisters, and now her own grandson. Life often seemed harsh, but today it seemed difficult to bear.

Jackson Msiko was a man of substance in the village, not just because of his age and experience or the fact that he had once owned many cattle, but because, although no-one could prove it or show the documents to support it, but he was man of history. He carried his tribe's history with him; he spoke with authority in his voice of the times when African culture and African civilization was as strong and sophisticated as anything in China or Europe. He spoke of a time before Gengis Khan, before Hannibal, before Ptolemy even, when the Kings of African nations had the greatest wealth, more cattle, more gold and more soldiers than anywhere in the known world. He remembered a time before independence when they were taught in school that white men discovered Africa and that Christian missionaries civilized them. Fortunately, nowadays a different perspective was taught, but still in schools no mention was made of the great empires of Mali or the kingdom of Shaka. He had tried to make amends and whilst his daughter had no time for him his granddaughter and her children would listen and carry these important histories forward.

Africa, it is true, needed the church. The Catholic church had arrived in his country over one hundred years ago at a time when Europeans were slaughtering whole villages. They offered peace and security and the greatest magic of all, education. This proved to be the strongest medicine, better than juju. In return Jackson's great-grandfather agreed to send his sons to church, to train to be priests. Today the church is the centre of village life, more than any government in Dar, more than any gift from America but it is still a European church.

Anna felt most at peace in the church. She had been cleaning the church for three years, one of a group of women who swept and washed and polished. Father Gerold was gentle, heard her confession each month and often had time to explain aspects of scripture or a difficult reading from Mass. She had been planning to join the choir for several months, but each Wednesday when she should go for practice her confidence ebbed and she stayed resting in the shade of her house.

The three of them sat in silence – the two women on a rough bench and Babu Jackson in the only armchair they possessed. As if sensitive to the moment, people calling from outside broke the uneasy silence. A number of voices seemed to become louder and then, like an unruly pet or an unwelcome breeze, a small boy burst into the dark space.
"It's Innocent. He's come home."
Anna looked at Rose; Rose looked at the empty space

between the door and the young intruder; Babu Jackson looked at his feet. He then sat back in his chair and chewed a short twig. After a few moments, he spat out the twig, took an old cloth from his trouser pocket and wiped his head; wiped his whole head. He pushed the cloth back in his trouser pocket and then as though suddenly remembering that he needed to be somewhere else, rose to his feet, stooped low through the doorway and was gone. Anna ran after him to see if it was true. She called back the young boy.

"Where? Where is he? Have you seen him?"

"I haven't seen him. My mum just told me that I should come and tell you."

Anna gathered her kanga around her and walked stiffly in the direction of town. Rose sat alone in the gloom, mosquitoes gathering now as the light quickly faded. She heard a noise outside, a rustling of cloth and a faint whisper.

"Hodi? Hodi?"

Rose gathered her kanga and called,

"Karibu". She knew the voice and moved quickly but painfully to the door. Innocent stood in the shadow of the house, his bulky figure clear in outline but his face unlit.

Rose stayed silent. Innocent spoke first.

"How are you? I waited until your mother had passed before I came. I understand that everyone knows about us now. Is your grandfather angry?"

Rose said nothing. She looked and she waited. She

wanted to speak but could neither think of the right words nor trust herself not to cry. Innocent pressed on,

"You know Rose, I didn't know. I would have called, but I didn't know."

"Well it doesn't matter now anyway. You're too late."

"I know. Someone just told me. The baby died. I'm sorry."

"Yes. Today. The baby died today. Who told you to come today?"

Silence. Innocent stared at the floor.

"Well, you're too late. And truthfully, you're not welcome. This place is not going to be gentle with you. Your mum has nothing and when Babu went to your home he came back with a very bad impression."

"Babu? Babu! This has nothing to do with him. If we were in Dar now, we'd live how we want. We'd have our own place and your grandfather could say nothing."

"If we were in Dar? You're dreaming. If life in Dar is so great why are you here?"

She was shaking but the light had faded and he couldn't see. They were two faceless shapes facing each other in the dark. Innocent waited; he wanted to say something, but he couldn't bring himself to the brink in time. If he had, he'd have said sorry. He'd have said how much he was pleased to be home, how many nights he'd thought of her, how much he regretted moving to Dar, away from his friends, his village, his place. At that moment, a small animal ran across the roof and she turned momentarily to look. Innocent, nervous, looking for a sign, assumed she was moving inside and at that same moment, turned and left. When Rose turned back to him, he was already several paces into the dark. The moment had passed. She saw an angry and impatient young man. He saw a grieving and unforgiving young woman.

Innocent went home to his village and his mother, who asked no questions, only served him food and cleared a bed for him. Before daylight the next morning, she rose as normal to go to her small-holding where she grew onions and tomatoes. Innocent heard her moving, waited for her to leave then quickly dressed and followed her. He took with him an old hoe from the house. It was light before they arrived at the field, his mother aware that he was following but still they did not speak. Only when she arrived at the place that she had left the previous evening did Innocent speak.
"You go for water mother. I'll take it over here." She looked at him, thought of asking him, put down her hoe and with a bucket on her head continued along the path to the small stream where she could collect water. Few men ever joined the women in the fields, least likely of all was her own son.

After some hours, he left his work and went to the stream to wash. He removed his clothes and hidden by the low hanging trees could wash his whole body in scooped handfuls thrown over his face. He was thorough in washing and was taken by surprise when he heard footsteps. He grabbed his trousers to cover himself.

"So. It's true. You are a farmer."

Rose had lost the harshness in her voice from the previous meeting. She seemed to sneer, but she gazed a little too long and Innocent knew she was no longer angry.

"How did you find me?"

"I wasn't looking for you if that's what you mean."

Innocent smiled.

"I have to pass this way to go to the clinic. It's a short-cut."

It was true. It was a short-cut to the clinic up on the hill; but still, it was a great and happy coincidence that she should pass as Innocent was washing himself.

Some hours later when she passed, returning from the clinic, Innocent was waiting for her. He sat on the side of the path with his hoe and jumped up as she appeared through the trees.

"Can I walk with you?"

"You don't go my way. Your home is over there."

"I know where my house is. I mean can I walk with you?"

She said nothing, but he moved alongside her and matched his strides to hers. Rose was tall; not as tall as Innocent, but she walked with long strides.

"Slow down. We're in no rush."

Rose smiled. She said nothing but shortened her stride slightly.

"Does it still hurt?", he asked. He realised he knew next to nothing about women's bodies or childbirth.

"It doesn't hurt so much anymore. The doctor says everything's fine. The baby probably got an infection and couldn't fight it. It might have been malaria. The doctor doesn't know." People here spoke of fate and God's will. His mother had spoken of the risks of modern medicine taunting God. If God wishes a baby to die who are we to deny him? He couldn't believe that. But the completeness of trusting God was something he had not experienced before. As the weeks passed, Innocent saw more clearly than ever that he could believe in some of this. He realised that he didn't need to believe like his mother, in the 'magic' of healing and spirits, but that if he worked hard in the fields and spent more time talking to old Father Gerold, he could begin to believe in God and his forgiveness. If he worked hard, cared for his mother and listened to old Father Gerold he might find a place in Rose's life again.

Chapter Eight

Great posters were going up all over town. Mbulu
had not seen so much colour on houses and shops for
many years – well, since the last election. A great
truck had pulled up in front of the District
Commissioner's office and four young men started
giving away kanga, leaflets, posters, even whistles.
Mr Jin, arrived at his office smiling brightly,
"Good morning, gentlemen. Great work. Good job."
The young men laughed and cheered. They offered
him a bright yellow peaked cap and for a moment he
tried it, offered them a great toothy grin and then
threw it back to them.
"Not today, eh, boys. Maybe later. We must be fair."

Many women that day were to be seen sporting the
bright yellow kanga emblazoned with the Party's
logo. That evening young men paraded through the
streets blowing their new whistles, their mothers
danced in their new yellow kanga and older men sat
on their plastic chairs and wondered if there would be
the same trouble this time round. Babu Jackson
passed one small group of old men. He too was
wearing the bright yellow baseball cap.
"Jackson. How is it?", one called.
"I'm fine thank you. How is that bicycle of yours? You
don't use it anymore? Too much beer?"

Everyone laughed. Jackson grinned and moved
quickly on, taking the steps up the District offices two

at a time. He was to see Jin about some land. He'd known Jin for years, had known his father and had at one time been thinking of marrying Jin's mother-in-law. That was long ago. Today, Jin was the senior officer in the DC's office and it was his permission he needed to buy the land. Strictly speaking, he could approach village elders and agree a price but without the DC's seal, the land could be identified for development without compensation.

"Good morning Mrs Ntile. How is the family?"

"Good morning to you Mr Jackson. They are fine, thank you. I hope all is well with you."

"You are looking particularly beautiful this morning. But I'm sure all those young men out there have already told you so."

Mama Ntile knew Babu Jackson as an old flatterer and never to be trusted, but she liked the fact that even she was worthy of his compliments, no matter how insincere. Being noticed mattered. You'd never be noticed if you wore the same garish kanga as all the other women, but then perhaps you didn't want to be noticed for not wearing it.

"If you take a seat I'll tell Mr Jin that you're here." She moved sluggishly from her chair, squeezing round the table and with a gentle knock on the door, into Mr Jin's office behind her.

Jackson had saved enough money to pay what he believed and the elders agreed would be a fair price for a plot of land in the village. Land outside the town of Mbulu was considerably cheaper and whilst it was not the best land for cultivation it was sufficiently far from the main road not to attract the attention of developers for some years to come. Once developers saw potential, planning applications were made, bribes were paid and permissions denied. No matter how well he knew Jin, everyone could be bribed.

"Good morning Willie," Jin's office smelt of the pungent oil he used after shaving. Jackson's hand would carry the stink all day. Jackson couldn't remember when Jin decided that he was old enough and with sufficient social standing to call him Willie and not Mr Jackson.

"How is the family? How is young Rose?"

Jin knew why Jackson had come. He wouldn't have been able to hold this job down for as long as he had without knowing other people's business. Jin listened as Jackson explained, drew from under his arm some sheets of paper – a large map, plans and a typed letter from the village elder – and pointed out to Jin where precisely the land boundaries would lie. This paperwork had cost Jackson a lot. Jin seemed to listen intently. As Jackson folded the paperwork, Jin smiled broadly and as he returned to his chair and folded his arms he looked squarely at Jackson

"And the usual considerations?"

"Of course, the usual considerations. Goes without saying."

"Everything seems to be in order to me, Willie."

Jin would need to do some work with Jackson's application. Nothing is ever purely bureaucratic. He paid a young man with a motorcycle to report back to him on local matters of every description. He paid him in beers and soda, but was rewarded in good bribes from much wealthier officials.

Jackson left the office, called a young man on a motorcycle over, after a word, stepped up and on to the pillion and sped off back to Anna and Rose with his news.

Town seemed to be covered in garish yellow – posters, flags and banners shouting, "Today is ours. Remember it." This sudden swamping of the town in yellow came the day after the first newspaper reports of a possible investment by a Chinese company. Hundreds of new jobs were to be created in a cement factory on the edge of town. It's what the town needed most. Jobs for young men. Jobs that would stem the leakage of young people leaving Mbulu to go to the bright lights and startling future everyone believed was theirs in Dar. There might be a job there for Innocent. He would never make a farmer, that's for sure.

The motorcycle was speeding down rutted tracks, past a primary school, its flagpole waving a limp and tattered national flag. Jackson patted the young rider on the shoulder and they stopped at a wooden street stall, a rickety table bearing some carefully stacked heaps of tomatoes, mangoes, a pineapple. A young woman perched on an upturned bucket picked her teeth with a sharpened stick. He bought two cigarettes and climbed back on to the motorcycle. Jackson noted the yellow streamers fluttering from the motorcycle's handlebars.

At home Anna was busy with a hen. The talk as she plucked and Rose swept was of the wedding. Rose and Innocent were to be married next month. The marriage would be celebrated by Father Gerold and he had agreed to let the village use the small kindergarten for the wedding feast. Two of her neighbours had agreed to help form a small organising committee to make sure that everything that should be done was done in time and at the best possible price. Jackson would know if they paid too much.

It had been almost exactly one year since Innocent had walked back to the village with Father Gerold. In that twelve months, Innocent had become an invaluable assistant to Gerold. He was always available to help with some minor repair to the house or the church. When Gerold was called on to help with a young family whose latrine had collapsed, Innocent was willing and able to dig a new pit. Early each Saturday morning Innocent led the young football team in their exercises – running, stretching and jumping. He was helping on Sunday afternoons with bible class, organising the tables and chairs in neat rows for the older parishioners to sit in the shade of the great mango tree.

"I spoke to Rose last night, Father – about the wedding," he'd admitted one morning as they took tea together.

"Good man! And what did she say? Was she pleased?"

"I think she was. She said she would speak to Babu about it."

"You should speak to him first! Tell her. You must speak to Jackson before she does. He'll like that."

"Rose is her own woman you know Father. Babu Jackson won't stop her nor make her do it if she doesn't want it."

"I know that. I think even Jackson knows that. But he will like it if you ask him. And things will run smoothly then. Believe me."

"Why should I believe you'll be any different this time?" Jackson had replied when Innocent finally spoke to him about Rose. "You left last time. And when she needed you, where were you? Up to no good in Dar. And then you only came home with your tail between your legs when things turned sour."

"I know Babu. I understand why it seems I shouldn't be trusted. But I believe I have changed. I'm not the same man I was then."

"You're hardly a man now," Jackson sneered. "And what of a bride price? That is out of the question I suppose."

"You know that I have nothing Babu. And my mother has even less. But I will work."

The conversation had ended there. Innocent told Rose about it later that day.

"He is right, Innocent. You left once. How do I know you will not do the same again?"

What could he say? Rose knew him better than he knew himself. She knew his weaknesses. She knew he was trying to be better. But she also knew how easily he could give in to temptation or give up when he met a problem.

"None of us can know what will happen. But I make you laugh better than anyone. We should be man and wife. And our next baby will grow big and strong."

Rose knew it too. The wedding was soon the celebration everyone in their village was talking about. There were celebrations every month for one thing or another – some young girls preparing for womanhood, young boys to be sent to the bush to prepare for manhood, a young man leaving for seminary, every week or so, a funeral. On each occasion there would be food, there would be sodas, sometimes beer. Always there would be Saturdays spent plaiting hair, preparing food, killing a goat. Always on Saturday mornings the streets would be filled with the blaring sound of bongo music from speakers bigger than some houses. Rose and Innocent's wedding was no different except that Babu Jackson would make sure it was the most talked about celebration this year.

Rose's dress was made from material bought in Dar. She went to a tailor in town who worked in a small block hut and had no fan. He had no electricity either so he didn't need a fan. But the hut had only one window and no breeze ever forced its way in. Rose hated going for fittings as she sweated so badly and was embarrassed when the material stuck to her flesh. "Don't worry, Rose," said Ally, the tailor. "You should see the fat ones. You are so beautiful. That boy will love you so much." It didn't make sense but Rose liked to hear it anyway.

There were to be bridesmaids and stewards. Each would wear the same design. It was a design of mustards and turquoise swirls. The sharp contrasts of Africa screamed from this design with its boastful plants and starbursts. Bridesmaids dresses, jackets and scarves. Everyone would wear the cloth Jackson had been to Dar to buy. Even the choir would wear a scarf made from this cloth. This wedding would not be forgotten. Jackson was the chairman of the organising committee but in truth he couldn't have arranged anything without the hard work of several women- Anna's friends and neighbours. Anna had few friends but many neighbours.

Anna seemed so confident with her neighbours. She was capable of giving orders, organising arrangements and making decisions. She was less comfortable taking advice or listening to complaints. "Don't worry," she would say, when the other women would come to her with a problem about the catering or the music or the electricity that so often had some problem or other. "Just stick to the jobs you have and everything will be fine."

As a child, Anna had been nervous and difficult. She had cried rather too much – so her mother had told Jackson once when he asked. She would never seem able to judge her mother's mood and her behaviour would often be met with a slap or a stick or at least a cruel word or two. Anna rarely cried though. She would laugh nervously and run off when she had been punished. But she wouldn't cry, not in front of her mother at least. She would run into the bush and hide in her favourite tree. It grew between some large rocks, the only rocks for some distance and an old gnarled tree had grown into a wondrous shape, twisting itself round the rocks and forcing its roots deep under so that the rocks and the tree had become one. Here, she could find small nooks in which to poke sticks where she'd find great beetles. She'd hide there all afternoon some days. She could never tell her mother what her father had done. She would never believe her and she'd be beaten soundly. She never spoke to other girls about it.

When she'd met the father of her first child, she was grateful for the short-lived affection, for the baby and for a home away from her mother. Her first child, Miriam, had died after two months. She remembered the pain in her breasts from the milk, unwanted, and the longing to smell the folds in her neck after she'd slept. Jacline had been the result of another one or two nights with a stranger – a soldier, posted to Mbulu, for three months. Rose had come some years later as a gift, she believed. She believed because the priest had assured her that a baby would come. The man she'd slept with did not care and nor did Anna. He was a traveller, a tall Masai, and Rose had his coppery features, long legs and self-assured nature.

She still lived in her mother and father's house with Rose. Her father had left after her mother died. He'd first moved to Dar to stay with his brother and start some business selling cars, but he'd returned a year or two later and now rented a tiny two-roomed house on the edge of the village. He had enough small enterprises to live comfortably. He rarely drank and he never borrowed and as a result, his savings had grown. He had a fine plot of land outside the village on which he raised cassava, bananas, tomatoes and maize. He had even tried his hand at rice but there was rarely enough rain. He owned a motorcycle which he rented to a young boy who paid him a few thousand shillings each day he used it. He'd spent several years in the army as a young man and now had a small pension for his trouble.

Why he favoured Rose more than his other grandchildren, no-one knew. People often mused but he rarely thought about it. Jacline had two sons - one had left home to join a religious order and the other worked in a bank in Mbeya. He rarely saw either of them. Rose's wedding was to be the first family celebration that for Babu Jackson meant anything at all.

Chapter Nine

Rose loved the early morning more than any other time of day. She loved to rise and light a fire, ready to make porridge for Innocent. But that would be in an hour or two. For now, she had time to herself; the morning, the cocks crowing and the sun rising. All this to herself. She swept the hard, red dirt from around her home. She fanned the fire and watched as the sticks first smouldered then a weak flame took hold and licked the big old pan resting on three charred stones. Bending over the fire was more difficult now. She had perhaps six more weeks before the baby was born. She hoped it would pass quickly.

Of course, she'd looked forward to this time as a young girl, perhaps for as long as she could remember. When her teacher and her grandfather talked to her as a young girl of all the things she could expect to achieve with her education, she'd dreamed of a house, a baby, a man asleep and food cooking on her very own pot. Already at her wedding she had learned that life wouldn't be as smooth. Her first baby had died and for the past months she'd worried most days that this baby, if it survived being born, would get sick and die. Her wedding had been a great celebration. It had been a huge success for her grandfather whose reputation had shone in the eyes of the sixty or so guests who had paid handsomely for the privilege of attending such a spectacle.

After the wedding, Rose and Innocent had made their home on the plot bought by Jackson earlier last year. Anna had arranged for a small traditional home to be built. Made of wattle and mud, with a thatched roof and a pit for a latrine, it was further from town than her mother's house but she had her own land. She already had some hens and was hoping next year to buy a goat. Innocent, with encouragement and even some help from Father Gerold, had marked, dug and seeded the land. The first green shoots of maize were pushing up. Cassava and tomatoes would follow.

Cock crowed and Innocent shouted from his bed, "Is porridge ready already?"
Always the same. Each morning he would call from his bed. Each morning he would fall back to sleep and have to be woken by Rose. When he did go to the field, he worked hard each morning. At least he worked until the rains started. With the rains came his excuses for going to town and looking for work. Rose saw him some days, smoking and laughing with boys and their motorcycles.

For Innocent, each morning he would wake with the best intention to work in the field, perhaps look for a job and help Father Gerold about his house and with the small jobs that needed doing around church. By the time the sun was up and the day was getting warm, however, he would often slouch off to town and see his friends leaning on their motorcycles, perhaps drinking a soda, another smoking a cigarette.

"Hi Innocent. Innocenti!" one would shout. "Come over here. Let me show you how to feed a baby." They'd laugh. He knew they were laughing at him but he was happy to be included in their jokes. Usually the talk would be about nothing. A man selling a motorcycle,

"What would be his best price?" Someone had got a new phone, second hand from young Medi on the market.

"It's the newer Samsung".

"Did you know there are jobs in Dar that pay four times what they pay here. We should go."

Sometimes an old Indian man with a big open-backed truck would pass and ask if they wanted work. They'd jump in, slapping each other and whistle to passing girls. They'd dig a road or a drain for a few hours and earn a few thousand shillings and walk back to town. They'd buy a cigarette or some chewing gum on the way.

Innocent felt comfortable in this company. He increasingly felt uncomfortable – anxious – when he faced the prospect of a day with Father Gerold, a meeting with Babu Jackson or even a day at home with Rose. He was beginning to realise that he couldn't plan his life. He was aware of stress, of anxiety that grew from nowhere and when he tried to plan or thought of all the ways his plan would not work, or how he couldn't stick to a plan, his anxiety would grow. On those days when he stayed at home working, he would lie in bed at night and every conceivable problem with every aspect of his plan for the coming days weeks or months would rattle around in his head until he found himself counting and trying to remember solutions he'd thought of yesterday but now couldn't remember. And when he couldn't remember he'd feel more anxious until he'd shake himself and remember that it was only a plan anyway, that it didn't matter because it wasn't going to happen. But then he'd close his eyes and it would all start over again. Often, he would lie, sleepless, turning, hoping that sleep would come. He'd fall asleep in the early hours to be woken by cocks crowing and Rose calling him.

Since the death of her first baby, Rose had helped in the office in the technical college. She made tea, swept the office and if the phone rang she would answer the phone. The phone never rang. But it was a job. Thanks again to her grandfather. Babu Jackson had had to go and see the Principal. The price of Rose's job was a young goat, given to Jackson in return for an introduction to the District Commissioner. The DC knew Jackson from his days in the army. At least that's what Jackson claimed and the DC was too proud to deny it, so when he asked him to meet his old friend Afthab, the DC agreed and Afthab was so pleased with the meeting he gave Jackson a young goat on the occasion of the President's birthday. Jackson did not know his own birthday but he knew the President's.

Rose would give up her job on the birth of the baby. The job did not come with the usual benefits of a government job. This was a private arrangement. She would work for the next few weeks until it became too difficult to manage the hill down to the college and then she would stay at home and wait for her baby.

As the weeks passed she realised that she cared less about what Innocent did or did not do and more about the health of her baby. She remembered all too clearly the pain of the loss of her first baby and cleaned and washed feverishly by way of preparation.

If she did go to the collection of shops on the outskirts of town she would search out the wooden stalls that sold used clothing. There she would rummage through some of the piles of clothes looking for small white things suitable for a baby. Of course, they were mostly adult clothes – T-shirts from Europe and America and blue jeans suspended with string on twigs made into coat-hangers that let the shirts and trousers flutter wildly in the wind. Baby items were harder to come by and she could not afford to buy new clothes.

She shouted Innocent one last time and then gathered her things, slipping on her sandals and wrapping her head in a shawl. She made her away from the small house at the edge of her field and down the rutted track to town. Before they had moved out to this more remote spot she would have been able to call on Janet. Janet had left school the year after Rose and, although like Rose, she had been quite studious, there were fees still owed to school and she had been unable to collect her school-leaver's certificate. Janet still lived with her mum in the small district, close to Anna. Rose sometimes envied her, but not often. Today, as she walked along the edge of the young maize shoots she felt pleased with her life. This plot would be a fine place to raise her baby.

As she approached college, some way to the west of town centre, she saw the yellow flags of the Government Party draped over the small hut that stood at the entrance to the college grounds. A makeshift barrier made from a broken tree was operated by two policewomen in blue skirts, bright white socks and shiny black shoes. They wore shiny white hats and carried braid across their chests to their shirt pockets. Their socks reached just up the centre of their calves and made their stout legs look so much fatter.

"Good morning ladies." She sang as she squeezed past their barrier and down the track to the college office.

"What's happening today? Whose are all those fine white cars?"

"Don't ask us. We're just told, 'Top Security for VIP' and 'Don't leave your post ladies.' "And they slapped their thighs and chuckled. "Big shots from Dar, I think. Maybe they are going to open that big factory the President was talking about."

It was not so unusual to see such visits at college. The college had the largest hall in the district capable of holding large gatherings for political rallies. Each year on the national holiday marking independence, the local MP or sometimes a government Minister would hold a feast for invited party workers and officials. It was renowned as the best event of the year. On one occasion, a cow had been killed to feed fresh beef to all the invited guests. Great white cars and slick black cars filled the driveway and blocked the road so that the local buses had to make the perilous journey through the houses and risk getting stuck in the thick mud after the rains.

After she'd made her way to her small desk at the back of the college office, Gervaise, her boss, told her to make tea in the big urn and wash plates ready to serve food. A delivery of heavy doughnuts had arrived and were to be served at the back of the hall to the guests as they arrived. The VIPs were in a separate meeting in the Principal's office and she should serve them tea and doughnuts first. Gervaise sat at his desk and seemed to be reading some papers which Rose was certain she'd seen on that same desk last week. He wore a newly pressed shirt and smelt of hair oil.

Now, to work! Ah. So much to do! Usually, she spent her time chatting to some of the staff, tidying papers or washing the front steps. Today, she would have to work hard and moving around had never been so difficult. She would take her time, no matter how important they were.

"....economic development means jobs for everyone." The speakers sitting on shelves on the wall of the great hall bounced in excitement as the crowd jumped to their feet and started shouting their applause. Great ululations from the women and the banging of plastic chairs with clenched fists in a hall with plain block walls provided an echo that hurt. The speaker stood at the microphone on the stage made of wooden tables, his fists clenched and held aloft in a powerful gesture of battle. Rose was straightening the cups and plates on the table at the rear of the hall, a stained plastic cloth served to hide the numerous marks and stains on the folding table. As the applause faded to a hum of chattering, a queue quickly formed as guests served themselves with the refreshments. A great bowl, sometimes used for washing hands, had been found to hold three bags of sugar. Two great flies gorged themselves between spoons

Rose listened to the snatches of conversation as guests moved slowly down the line past the doughnuts on to the tea and finally reached the sugar. Women, few she recognised, wearing bright African colours, many of them with matching headdress spoke of promotions, whispered about children, about men. Another complained about the allowances her boss had denied her,

"How does he think we will manage?"

Men in dark suits, white suits, others in Muslim kameez and kufir – all shuffled by talking excitedly of the new investment to come and what it might mean for their bank, for their school, for their department. One old man smiled at Rose and asked her when her baby was due.

"Next month. God willing," and curtsied.

As the guests departed, the VIPs and their drivers sped down the driveway in clouds of dust and young men started rewinding the meters of cable that had fed the sound system, Gervaise pulled her roughly to one side.

"Did you hear what the Minister said?" Rose hadn't known that he was a Minister.

"I heard them talking about jobs. What does it mean?"

"Yes. Jobs for some. Their families no doubt. But the factory will be sited just south of Ulungu. All that land will be marked for government use."

Rose stared blankly. She didn't mean to appear blank, but she didn't know what to say.

"My family's land will be taken and I will receive nothing."

Rose was about to make a sympathetic noise, but Gervaise pre-empted her

"Yes. Old Babu Jackson must have known a thing or two. You're ok aren't you. I'm happy for you." His face told a different story.

"But there will be compensation?"

"Worthless. They can do what they want so they pay next to nothing."

That evening Babu Jackson came to Rose's house. He'd brought over another hen, tied to his motorcycle. "Here. Rose. Take this. It's the only one left from old man Paulo. The rest died."
"Thanks Babu. I have pills to help stop that disease."
Her first batch of hens had died before they had given any eggs. She was careful to speak to the man at the market about possible pills and cures. Babu sat down in the one chair they possessed, under the shade of the roof as it overhung the house giving a cooler spot in the heat of the day. It was dark now but the red dirt was still warm to touch.
"Why did you not go the big meeting with the Minister, grandad?"
"I was there. I just didn't stay for tea. I needed to speak to the DC before he left with the others. Where's Innocent?"
"He's in town. He has just gone to buy some small things. He was working hard in the field this afternoon," she lied.
Jackson searched her face but could see little in the dark and he said nothing.
"Tell him that I need to speak to him."
"What have you got to tell him? Whatever it is you can tell me. You should tell me."
"He needs to speak to me. There will be an announcement about the new factory and he should be first in line. But he must see me."

"I'll tell him."

Innocent came home quite late, after Rose had gone to bed. He heard him from yards down the track and as he stopped to enter the house he knocked the table. Their home had three rooms. In the centre of one room was a table; in one corner stood a cupboard Innocent had made from some offcuts of wood he'd found in town and on one wall sat a shelf for papers, keys and other important things. In one other room was their bed, a gift at their wedding and to one side a wooden chest for clothes and bedding. The other room stored a bicycle and farming equipment – a hoe, a sharp blade and some other smaller items used for cultivation. As their children grew, if they hadn't moved from this house, this room would be a child's bedroom and more storage would need to be built outside. The house was roughly built so that on the side of the room where Innocent slept sharp ends of sticks protruded through the mud walls. Innocent regularly forgot this, especially when he'd had beer, and scratched himself. Tonight, as he scratched his head in bending to remove his trousers, he swore loudly. Rose lay still and silent. She would know from his breathing when he'd gone to sleep and she would only roll on her side once she knew he had done so.

She woke with the hens. For the time being she kept them in the second room and she was quick to let them out once she'd heard them rustling. The first hour or two was noisy as their one cockerel chased one hen then another, pinning her down at the neck, mounting her, then crowing loudly, enough to wake Innocent. Rose had fetched water from the standpipe a few hundred yards from their house. Jackson had worked harder and spent more on bribes to get that water tap than he had to secure the purchase of the land. Without water, their life would be hard. Rains only came for a few weeks a year and they had not means to store enough rainwater for all their needs. She stored water in a large plastic bin with an ill-fitting lid to the rear of the house. Innocent would stand there with a small jug to wash himself. She always took pleasure in watching him wash, no matter how late he'd come in the night before.

As he ate his porridge, Rose told him of Jackson's visit the night before
"I think he must have news of some jobs. He says you can be first in line."
"You know Rose, I'm not sure I want to work in an office in that factory. And who's to say when it will be built."
"It will be built now for sure. Too many people know about it and too many people are banking on it for their future for the government to change its mind now."
"That may be true, but I'm still thinking I should try and run my own business. I was going to ask Babu for a loan."
"I don't want to be there when you ask. He will laugh at you. That's if he doesn't beat you."

"Beat me? Do you think so? Do you think he'd dare? Beat me, you say?"

He went off carrying his hoe over his shoulder, looked back at Rose from the top of the field and spat. Rose went to college as usual and when she returned Innocent had gone, his hoe leaning against the house.

Father Gerold came to visit her that afternoon. He was sweaty and tired. He drank a cup of water and sat in the shade offered by the roof of the house. A small flame tree some yards away would offer better shade in time, but it had some years to grow before one might sit beneath its branches.

"I saw Innocent in town just now. He is smoking with his pals by the bus stand. Does he think that will help provide for this baby when it's born?"

"I know Father. I tell him. I try to talk to him but he is not himself recently."

Rose knew that this was a lie. Innocent was no different to the young boy who'd gone to Dar over two years ago.

"I've come to tell you that one of the women who cleans the church, Mama Stefano, you might remember her? She has some baby things for you. She wants no money but will take them back when the baby outgrows them."

"Tell her that I'm very grateful. I will go and see her later."

Rose knew that this was the reason for Father Gerold's visit. The priest did not struggle up this lane to her house to tell her about baby clothes.

"I have a favour to ask, Rose." Gerold had made himself comfortable on the seat in the shade. "There is a young family in difficulty. The father has left and sends no word nor money and the mother is ill. There are three children. The grandmother will take two of them but the older one will be too much for her."

"Ill, you say? What is the problem?"

"They don't say but I suspect she has HIV. She has become so ill and so thin so quickly, it's what everyone says, but only in whispers."

Everyone knew of the threat from HIV and yet few spoke openly. Gerold was one of the few men – and a priest too! – who would broach such a subject openly, and with a woman.

"What can I do? We have so little ourselves." Her legs were stretched out in front of her as she leaned back against the cool wall of the house, it being the only position in which she could sit in relative comfort with her baby so close to its due date.

"The girl is called Sarah. She is thirteen and she needs a home. Very soon you will need help and she is capable."

"But we have barely enough to feed ourselves…"

"You have enough. And you have a family to help. I know you will do this Rose. It is a blessing."

It was true that a girl to cook and clean would be a big help. It would also mean that she could go back to work sooner than she had planned…What was she thinking? She hadn't even met the girl. Would she really leave her baby with a stranger and a young teenager at that? Father Gerold was already getting up to go.

"I'll leave you to discuss this with Innocent and you can come to church to give me your answer tomorrow."

By the time Innocent came home that night, Rose had made her decision and heaved herself down to church the next day before going to college to tell Father Gerold.

"Good. I knew it. I will tell the girl, Sarah. She will bring her things to you in the coming days."

"Father. What about her school? Is she not to go to school?"

"She will complete Standard Seven this year. The grandmother has no money for her to continue to secondary school. And besides, you need her to work in your home."

The decision was made and the young girl, Sarah, arrived at Rose's house on Saturday morning, carrying a large plastic zipped carrier bag emblazoned with a colourful map of Africa and boasting a selection of pictures of Africa's 'Big Five'. In the bag, she had a dress, some knickers, socks, a pair of school shoes, a blanket and a hairbrush. She carried the bag with deft confidence on her head and on her arm she carried a bucket in which she carried a cup and a bowl. Rose and Sarah set to work clearing the second room, making space for a bed, or at least a space for the girl to sleep. The hoe and other tools could stay in the corner; the bicycle would take its chances outside, hidden from view.

The girl was slight, dark skinned with closely cropped hair. She was short for her age, or at least shorter than Rose at the same age and Rose quickly noticed that she had a habit of inclining her head slightly when listening, as though she were either listening intently or preparing to sneer. Rose wasn't sure whether this irritated her or not.

"Why do you hold you head like that when I'm speaking?". Rose worried momentarily if she had been too harsh.

"Sorry, Mama. It's just a habit."

"No matter. And I am Rose or dada, sister. I'm not your mama. What have you to do today?"

"I've to take food to my mum up at the hospital. My grandmother has been going each day but she needs help."

"Good. I will give you some small things to take with you. Be sure to be back here before dark."

Sarah had set off for hospital before Innocent was awake. When she returned Innocent was in town and so it was Sunday morning before Innocent and Sarah met. They were dressing for church and Sarah was waiting for them outside. She wore her shiny black shoes and white socks and was chasing the hens into the house with a stick. Innocent sometimes missed Mass, having stayed up late the night before, but today he was up and dressed before Rose. Rose could no longer wear her best dress on account of the pregnancy but covered her working dress with a bright clean kanga. Sarah greeted Innocent with a smile and a curtsy,

"Good morning. You are our new house girl?" Innocent knew how foolish this sounded as he had never dreamt that he would have a house girl.

The three of them set off slowly down the track to church. It was much further to church from this their new home than it had been from her mother's home. Rose and Innocent made their way slowly in silence. When they arrived, the church was already nearly full, the choir in full song and the priest and servers on the altar. Sarah and Rose eased their way in to a pew, other women shuffling along to make room. Innocent took a pew with the men. All around him men sang in strong tuneful voices. Innocent mouthed the words, but made so sound.

After Mass, Sarah went to chat with some of her friends. They wanted to know about her new home and ask about her mother. Rose waited outside the presbytery for Father Gerold. As soon as he appeared he asked for Innocent.

"He's already gone, Father. He seems so unhappy at the moment. I can't understand his mood." Gerold paused, waiting for the right words.

"I will try and speak to him but he avoids me too. At least you have Sarah to help you now."

Rose scoffed, "I don't need Innocent to care for me.

It's him I'm worried about."

Chapter Ten

As Innocent waited at the bus stand, Rose and her mum were struggling up the hill to hospital. It was still dark but the heat was sticky. Her waters had broken and the pains were stronger by the minute. Rose had wanted to stay at home but Anna had insisted and for once her insistence had overpowered Rose,
"This baby will have a better chance if it's born with a doctor present."

Innocent had borrowed the bus fare from a friend. The friend laughed when Innocent had said that he'd pay him the following week,
"Are you sure you'll be back, Innocenti? I have the feeling you'll be away for some time."
"No. Not at all. What do you mean? I'm just going to see my brother about some work he needs some help with. I'll be back next week for sure. And I'll have money to pay you. But I'll call you, whatever."
Innocent wondered sometimes how easily he could lie. He hadn't had to think too hard. The stories tripped off his tongue so smoothly, he almost believed them.

He found a seat in the centre of the bus. Seats over the wheels were the least comfortable. He placed his cloth satchel in the seat next to him in the hope that it would remain vacant. In the glare of the strip light Innocent watched the young boy loading the bags and cases into the hold. The doors of the hold were to be strapped with rope. The driver was about to take his seat when an older man from the office called him over,

"Jacob. I need you take the later bus. The boy can take this one."

"Are you sure? He will need someone with him. He will get lost in Dar for sure."

"Don't worry about that. I have a young boy who will meet him on the way and guide him in."

The driver climbed down and the boy who had been loading the cases replaced him. The bus quickly filled up with old and young – young women off to see their aunts and sisters, old men to see an inspector about some land issue, a family of mother and four young children to a funeral in Mwanza, two days' journey from Mbulu, a smartly dressed man with a laptop, and many, many more, sixty-two seats and all of them filled. Innocent moved his satchel to make way for a large woman of probably fifty years. She forced one large carrier bag between her legs and another in the narrow space above her head. The bus pulled away with a roar, a blast on its boastful horn and a cloud of dust. The dark sky turned to a pale grey light; shaky wooden stalls selling juice, water, samosa and cakes were clouded out of sight and as the dust settled young boys ran after the bus through the dirt, waving their bright yellow flags and hats.

The first sign that there might be cause for concern

was when the driver, spending too long trying to select a music track, causing him to take his eyes off the road, swerved dangerously close to the unmade edge of the road. An older man near the front shouted at him sharply to take more care and drive more slowly but the boy turned around and grinned broadly,
"Don't worry old man. This is not just the fastest bus to Dar, it's also the safest."

The bus tore through small villages with tiny mud houses clinging to the edge of the road, mothers clasping their babies and old men holding their hats as the wind tried to whip them from their grasp. Young boys waved madly with one hand, holding their old bicycles in their other. On any occasion, the bus had to overtake another vehicle, the young driver would lean forward to press the horn and scare the cyclist or the small delivery vehicle to a stop. At every turn passengers on one side of the bus would lean into the aisle, holding firm to the seat in front. At first the women thought it great fun. They called to one another to hold tight and laughed in each other's faces. The young driver, Cedric, seemed to grow in confidence the more mirth he created. He was now braking viciously and taking bends at speeds that threw bags from the shelf overhead so that one emptied its contents in the aisle causing onions and socks and some plastic clothes pegs to roll around in the dirt on the floor.
"Slow down, man!", shouted one woman from the

rear of the bus. "You're going to kill us."

Innocent had never learned to drive – few passengers on this bus would have a driving licence – and he was possibly unaware of how dangerously close to collision the driver came each time he overtook a vehicle. Regardless of the bends in the road or the distance between this coach and the oncoming vehicle, the young driver obviously believed that an oncoming vehicle would get out of the way. At every bend, he was never sure what he would meet in the road in front. On one occasion, many passengers were thrown forward, some bumping their faces on the seat in front as the driver applied the brakes to slow to a stop to avoid some children on bicycles, unseen round the bend in the road.

An older woman made her way slowly and painstakingly to the front of the bus. She told everyone she passed how this had to stop,
"He is going to kill us. We should stop the bus and get off. We can wait for the next bus."
"Sit down," one replied. "The next bus will be full. Do you want to be stranded out here for the animals to eat you?"
"Animals!" another laughed. "There hasn't been a lion or leopard in these parts for many years."
"Not lions or leopards," said another. "But we've seen plenty of snakes. Last month my son helped to kill a giant python with a body thicker than my thigh."
"And elephants...", but before he could finish telling

us about elephants, the bus started braking, a coach approaching at speed in the opposite direction could not give way and the bus to Dar had to swerve. The old woman was hurled forward and thrown against the window at the front of the bus. The bus shuddered and shook, bags flew from one side to the other, a young child slid at speed down the central aisle, and then slowly, the bus started to lean and then tilt. It leaned slowly at first but once it had reached its tipping point it rolled. The coach rolled and splintered and crashed into bushes and small trees. Innocent's ankles were gripped by the bar under the seat in front. It seemed his feet would break from his ankles. The pain was severe and he screamed. He couldn't be heard above the screams and shouts, but these desperate screams were matched by the painful screeching of metal on road and the breaking of glass. He was held at one point upside down by his ankles trapped under the seat. As the bus came to a stop on its side, Innocent was trapped against the broken glass and the grassy ground, his fellow passenger on top of him. The shouting had stopped and now babies crying and people separately calling "Help!" and "My head" or "Here! Help!" were all that could be heard.

Innocent lay there for some minutes, trying to get accustomed to the pain. He felt liquid running across his neck. He couldn't see his neck because of the angle of his head but the warmth spread from his neck across his chest. The warmth was dark and, when it reached his t-shirt, red. The woman's head was twisted and she was silent. As he forced his head towards her face, he saw a metal pole protruding from the front of her neck. Blood oozed round the pole, across her face and soaked his chest.

The doctor had been called. No-one knew when she'd come. She'd delivered three babies that night She'd only just gone home and the administrator had sent a text to ask if she'd come back for an extra shift. Two nurses attended the long line of beds on each wall of the maternity ward. Thirty beds in total, twenty of them occupied. The nurses in their pale green uniforms seemed bored and tired. A woman wailed from the far end of the ward and one nurse called out to her,
"Be quiet, Mary. We are busy."

Rose and Anna were making themselves comfortable. Anna moving a pillow to help Rose take a position that might ease the pain. It was not light yet and the harshness from the strip light was keeping the woman in the neighbouring bed awake. One nurse, the quieter of the two, a short plump woman of perhaps twenty-five, switched off the light. It was light enough to see, if not to see clearly each other's faces, to see what was needed.
"I prefer that," said Rose. "I might sleep."
"I don't think you'll be sleeping, girl. The pain will come back soon enough. You'll see."
They remained together in silence; Rose, lying flat, trying to understand what each pain or ache from her

abdomen meant; Anna, sitting in the hard plastic chair to her side, stony-faced, holding her daughter's hand, staring at the wall. A hush fell over the ward as the moaning stopped with the only sound being the gentle snoring from the far end. It lasted a moment or two and then the moaning started again. The hours passed and Anna went outside to the small stalls on the street to buy some small cakes and a bottle of water. Rose slept for a few minutes at a time. Anna tried to sleep in the chair but her lolling head woke her.

Mid-afternoon, it started raining - great greedy drops of water smashing into the tin roof. The hospital ward sounded like the inside of a drum with a thousand tiny fists banging outside. There was no glass in the windows and the flimsy coloured curtains thrashed wildly. When the rain stopped, it stopped as I started, with a flourish. The drum just stopped, in a beat. As the sun forced a crack through the heavy clouds, so wisps of steam rose from the flags outside the hospital ward. Rich red rivulets ran between the cracks in the flags and formed great puddles by the door. The sun appeared only briefly. Soon it fell dark and another shift started.

The light was switched on as a tall woman in a white coat marched down the ward.
"Which one is Rose Msiko?" Anna stood and waved.
"She is here."
The doctor wasted no time in greetings but pulled

back the covers and felt Rose's belly. Rose flinched at the doctor's cold hands.

"How often are the contractions?" she asked Rose's belly. Rose and Anna looked at each other wondering who should answer.

"Every five or ten minutes," said Anna.

The doctor wrapped a strap round Rose's arm and noted her blood pressure on the sheet hanging on a card suspended from a nail in the wall above her bed.

"Everything seems fine. Come and get me, nurse, when we have some movement."

And with that the doctor marched away, the tails of her white coat flapping to keep up.

Within ten minutes of the doctor and both nurses leaving the ward, Rose's pain started again.

"They seem worse this time. You'd better get the doctor Mama."

Anna went to the door at the end of the ward to look. She could see no-one. She called weakly, afraid to disturb this orderly place. Still no-one came. She returned to Rose's side. Rose's face was now twisted in pain and she had positioned herself with her knees up and her thighs apart.

"I can feel it now. I'm going to push."

"Can't you just wait a moment or two. They'll be here soon I'm sure."

Rose ignored her and gripped the bed. She twisted the sheet in her fist. Small beads of sweat shone on her forehead. Anna threw back the sheet to see the baby's head clearly. Rose screamed, not loudly at first but then full-throated and deep as the nurses at first walked then ran to her bedside. They shouted and prodded but Rose knew what was to be done. She could feel the moment to push. One of the nurses expertly turned the head with one hand, held its slithery body with the other whilst the other nurse deftly cut the grey spindly cord. Moments later, the tiny boy, wrinkled, wet and coppery like his mother was wrapped tightly in a white sheet and lay on his mother's chest. The doctor swept past some minutes later and stopped long enough to record the time and weight on the crumpled sheet above Rose's head.

"What will you call him Rose?" her mother asked.

"I've no idea. I keep thinking of names but then I think I should ask Babu. There might be a family name we should use." Anna grimaced. Rose saw it.

"With that rain today, I thought we were going to be flooded. You should call him Noah," said one nurse. They all laughed.

"Noah." Rose weighed the sound of it. "Yes. That's his name. Noah."

Innocent had to press the dead woman's head out of his neck to make room to climb over her. To make his way to the front of the bus where the missing windscreen gave easy egress, he first had to climb over numerous bodies. His feet squashed legs, faces, babies' arms as he made his way through the wreckage. Smoke was seeping from near the driver's seat; above his head the parcel shelf hung incongruously, draping passengers' intimate belongings for the world to see.

Outside two men were carrying an old woman to a grassy patch some yards from the coach. He joined them and one patted his shoulder,
"Are you OK brother? You can walk"
"I think I'm OK. What should we do?"
"There will be more survivors in there. We just have to go and find them."
The three of them walked slowly round the coach listening, asking, feeling. They found a young woman clutching her baby. She was covered in clothing and an old man, dead, was pressing her into the seat, but she and her baby were unharmed. Innocent and the other man dragged the old man first through the open window and took her baby from her. The baby started to cry and his mother shushed him from her seat. With her arms free she could wrench herself free from the confines of the wreck.

By the time help had arrived to help pulling people from the wreck of the coach, nine bodies were already lined up on the roadside. A police vehicle with four men arrived and carefully set out fluttery tape to mark the spot. Only five adults including Innocent, were capable of helping with this work. But not the police. The bodies included two children, one with a crushed head, another who appeared unmarked but was dead when they'd found her. A Landcruiser with two white men passed. It slowed to view the wreckage and Innocent waved madly to ask them to stop. As he ran towards the car, it sped up and raced off down the hill.

"They think we want to hurt them. That's what all the wazungu are told when they visit this country. 'Don't stop your car for the natives', they're told."

"They will be punished for such harshness," Innocent replied.

When a bus eventually arrived from Mbulu, the dead and the injured were loaded aboard and taken back to Mbulu. Innocent and some of the others joined the dead and the wounded and hitched a lift home.

The next day the papers as well as the TV news carried the story,

'COACH DISASTER - NINETEEN DEAD, FORTY INJURED'

Innocent ached; his ankle hurt so much he walked gingerly, unable to put weight on his right leg. He'd suffered no cuts but he still wore the blood-stained t-shirt. That night he didn't go home. He drank some beer, smoked local hash with some strangers near the bus stand and slept in a wooden store whose flimsy lock had been forced. He awoke in the night and cried like a baby.

Chapter Eleven

When Innocent eventually made it home, it was to a home full of women. Rose, her mother, her friend Aisha and several neighbours were busying themselves with cleaning and cooking. Anna sat with the baby on a chair borrowed from a neighbour in the large room indoors, whilst two neighbours cooked ugali in the shade outside. Anna greeted Innocent as did the neighbours but no-one asked where he'd been or made any reference to the coach accident. Innocent realised that they had either not heard of the accident or not realised that he'd been involved. They assumed that he'd disappeared and now come home. No explanation was possible or expected. He sat in the bedroom briefly with Rose and the baby.

"Where have you been, Innocent? I just don't understand." Innocent held the baby's tiny fingers in his and stroked his face.

"Did you hear about the coach accident? It was terrible – so many bodies."

"I did not know Innocent. I'm sorry. Where have you been? I thought you were in Dar."

"I haven't been to Dar. I've been looking for work here in Mbulu. I'm sure things will be better once the factory opens."

"Babu says he can help. Will you see him?"

"Maybe. But I have some other contacts that can help too."

"Innocent, I will not be working for some weeks now and we have to have some money. What will we do?"

"Don't worry. It will be fine."

"Don't worry? Don't worry? The baby is well and so am I. But you didn't care enough to be here." Innocent stared at the baby.

"I have to see someone. I'll be back with some money tomorrow."

He changed his shirt and went out.

Rose called to him. The women stared after him as he left.

"Let him go. He is nothing," snarled one neighbour.

When he reached the bend in the track just before it sloped down to the road he turned to look back at his home. A mango tree some yards away framed the picture of women preparing food, wisps of smoke drifting up and young shoots of maize lining the path to his house. As he turned he felt more clearly than ever that he was looking at someone else's life, that he was a visitor, a pretender, a fraud. His life was somewhere else and he needed to return to feel that same sense of completeness that he'd felt when he'd first worked for Father Gerold. He wasn't sure what had happened to make this change in his mental state like this, but the strong sense of living someone else's life left him with a strong urge to run.

He ran down the track and down the road towards town. One of his pals from the bus stand passed on a motorcycle and stopped to give him a lift. He hoped on and enjoyed the wind in his face but mostly he enjoyed not being able to speak. He left his pal in town and started to walk towards his mother's home, a walk of just less than an hour. After half an hour, he stopped. He met some children playing in a small stream that ran between the two villages. Father Gerold's church stood on the small hill above the stream and between the two villages. Innocent drank as the children quizzed him

"What is your name?"

"Innocent," he replied.

"Where are you from?"

"From here. This is my home."

"We've never seen you before. Where do you live?"

He thought about the question and rather than answer he bent his arms into the water and splashed them, causing them to run and laugh. As he left they were splashing each other and had forgotten him completely. He walked, first to the church. Father Gerold was away and the church seemed abandoned. He walked around the priest's house if anyone was there or if a door had been left unlocked. If he could get in, Father Gerold would not mind him staying there. The doors were locked. He retraced his steps back to the main track and took the path towards his mother's house and called on Gertrude, one of Gerold's cleaners. She was at home, sleeping.

"Yes. I have a key. If you borrow it, you must return it. Father will be back tomorrow. Will you keep the key until then?"

Innocent returned to the priest's house and unlocked

first the iron grill, then the main door. There was no food in the house but he could sleep well on Gerold's great red sofa. As he closed his eyes to sleep the feeling of panic he'd felt so often before swamped him. There seemed to be no pattern. He could not see what triggered this feeling of otherness. He knew that the local weed he smoked with the boys at the bus stand calmed him like nothing else. Part of him knew that this was irregular, abnormal, not him; but a stronger part of him couldn't escape the sensation of the world, every thought, every movement rushing at such speed that he felt on the edge of an explosion. He lifted his hand to test whether his body was racing or if his mind was tricking him. He watched his hand move above his head. It looked normal but in his head every fraction of an inch was moving at lightning speeds. He leapt off the sofa and walked. When he walked, his head stopped racing.

He tried again to sleep but as soon as he closed his eyes his mind started racing again. If he had had to describe the feelings, he wouldn't say fear but the sense of being totally alone was close to fear. The feeling of being alone was stronger than any series of sensible thoughts he might have. Had he considered friends and family he might reasonably have considered himself to be friendless, but the strong sensation of being bombarded by speed, by every thought, every item around him, the hand at the end of his arm rushing towards him or rushing away from him left him so anxious that there was no room for reason. He wanted to run but felt too anxious. He wanted to sleep but felt too anxious. He considered stopping breathing but couldn't. He considered making the journey back to town to see if he could find some weed to smoke. He walked again – this time further. Again, he returned to the priest's house. He knew it was important that he remained alone.

Finally, after what felt like longer but had in fact been less than fifteen minutes, the anxiety and feeling of uncontrollable speed subsided and as he closed his eyes his heart rate eased and the sense of panic was replaced with that of exhaustion. He slept.

When Gerold returned the next day at around midday, Innocent was still asleep.
"House sitting is it, Innocent? Very kind. Not many burglars can be bothered to traipse out here. Easier pickings in town for them."
Innocent smiled. He knew that he didn't need to explain to Gerold.
"Rose was worried that you'd left for good. Did you hear about the accident on the road to Dar?"
"I was on that coach Father. It was terrible."
"You should have gone to hospital. I'm sorry Innocent. How have you been?"
"I've been fine. I'm glad I don't have to speak to all the families of those that died. So many mothers and fathers, brothers and sisters who will be weeping these days."
"I have three funerals this week. You can help if you

are able."

Innocent looked away. He felt a coward. He felt like he did when he hid in the bush as the robbers attacked the lorry driver. Why could he not offer to help? After all he'd survived. He should be grateful. But he only felt small. The thought of attending the funeral of one of the victims of the accident he survived made him want to make himself small. He stared at the floor and slowly drew his knees up and as he leaned into the sofa, slowly folded himself into as small a shape as he could make.

Gerold sat at the opposite end of the sofa and ignored Innocent's anguish.

"I know Babu Jackson has plans for a job for you. Will you speak to him?"

From underneath his folded arms Innocent's voice was muffled.

"Yes. I will go tomorrow. Not today."

"I heard some worrying news yesterday. I've been to see the bishop's secretary. The DC had been to speak to the bishop and the Chinese investment was discussed. The DC thinks it might not happen now."

Innocent lifted his head.

"You mean there might not be a cement factory?"

Gerold nodded, "I know. It's incredible. But the DC thinks they will pull out of the deal."

"After everything the President and all the Ministers have promised."

They both sat in silence, Innocent shaking his head and Gerold rubbing his.

"So is it the Chinese fault or the government's?" Innocent eventually turned to ask Gerold.

"Who knows? And it doesn't really matter. The government will try and blame the Chinese whoever's at fault."

"And who knows this? Does Babu Jackson know? You've just asked me to go and see him about a job."

"I know. I doubt if Jackson knows. And it won't harm to go and see him. As I say, as far as I know there has been a conversation between the DC and the bishop. But for the bishop's secretary to tell me... I think it's likely to be true."

Innocent said nothing. This revelation was important. Innocent did not know how or why, but from Gerold's weighty manner, his estimation of Jackson's reaction and the reaction of all those weed smoking boys at the bus stand, Innocent considered it wise to consult with others. He knew that this was likely to be the biggest news to affect Mbulu in some time.

Chapter Twelve

Opposite the bus stand was Mr Mkonga's hardware shop. Mr Mkonga was a short, dark skinned man wearing a permanent grin who, when he spoke, only complained. He complained about prices, about thieves, about the government about the weather. He complained about foreigners, about rich people in Dar and about poor people from Mozambique. He complained that nothing ever changed and he complained that things were always better when he was a child. He owned and ran a small store next to a similar shop selling mobile phones and next to another selling 'Small Bites'. The three shops formed a small terrace sitting on a raised concrete veranda supported by concrete steps. In front of this veranda stood a large mango tree that had not produced fruit for many years but provided shade for the innumerable bicycles, motorcycles and *tuck-tucks* waiting to transport people and goods from the bus stand or the market. It had long been an unofficial venue for public meetings, the veranda providing a natural vantage point from which to address a noisy, reluctant or unruly crowd.

Michael Zuhura, local chairman of the People's Party, the Party that had ruled the country since independence and which had enjoyed ninety percent support in every election since that time, had risen early that morning, taken his exercise, washed and eaten before dressing in a clean pressed white shirt, a bright yellow tie bearing the Party logo, blue trousers, brown belt and shiny new pointed black shoes. As he dressed he rehearsed a speech he had been constructing in his head since the phone call last night. He splashed hair oil to his head and face and shouted his departure to his wife and mother in the back of the house. Outside two younger men waited beside an old white Nissan with deep velour seats. Michael sank back into the back seat as the car left pulled away, tyres throwing up dirt and dust in its wake.

Mkonga knew nothing of the decision to invest or not invest, he knew nothing of the Party's public position and he knew nothing of the speech to be given that morning in front of his shop. He'd returned from mosque as usual, set out the coloured buckets, dismembered hoes, a great drum of kerosene which he sold by the litre in plastic water bottles and the dozens of other household items he'd set out for the last four years since he'd managed to secure the lease on his new shop. He was drinking his sweet tea with chapatti prepared by his wife in the kitchen at the rear of the shop when he heard a group of young boys shouting,
"Someone will pay for this." Mkonga looked over the top of his newspaper and saw a group of two or three men from his mosque engaging the boys in conversation. The shouting stopped as they listened intently. One of the young boys in jeans then threw his arms in the air wildly. Mkonga couldn't hear what

was said but he could see expression of angers on young faces with older men in kufirs looking on calmly. One old man, Juma, held out his arms, calling them back. The young boy turned his back and slammed his fist into the seat of his motorcycle.

The old white Nissan arrived in the small side street beside Mkonga's shop being driven too fast and came to a halt with tyres sliding in the dry dirt. The two boys in the front quickly made their way to Mkonga's shop
"We have to move this stuff, old man. Comrade Zuhura is going to speak and there will be a crowd."

They began dragging Mkonga's wares back into his shop. Mkonga folded his paper and took his teacup into the shop. When he returned, the boys were trying to get a grip on the kerosene.
"Careful with that drum. If that falls we will have one hell of a mess."
Mkonga knew not to object. He also knew that if he moved slowly, these two bucks would do all the heavy work. While they worked, the owners of bicycles motorcycles and the daladala had moved them to a safer spot at the side of the bus stand.

At no point that anyone could discern and without audible sign the crowd gathered; slowly at first as the bicycles were removed, and then, with something like a slow tide creeping forward, women and men alike, older men to the edges, keeping their distance, older women in the centre, shouting to their friends and neighbours, the mixed population of Mbulu or at least a good cross section of life there, gathered in front of Mkonga's shop. Mkonga's shopfront was closed and as a final act of caution he swung his wooden shutters round to close. Hopefully, he could re-open in an hour or two. Michael Zuhura stepped on the to the veranda from the side street. He wore dark glasses and a yellow peaked cap. Parts of the crowd fell silent. One man from the centre of the crowd shouted, "Comrade. Let's hope you have good news."

One of Michael's young helpers stepped up with a handheld loudspeaker. It squeaked as he switched it on.

"Comrades, brothers and sisters. First of all, our President, Comrade Elimu, sends his greetings. He would be here today but he is, as we stand here, meeting important heads of state from Europe and America. He has asked me to convey to you his personal greetings. You, I know, support him in his daily work to ensure that European and American leaders fulfil their promises to us." Some cheers and ululations started and almost immediately petered.

"He is aware, as you are, that this country needs to continue on the path of sustainable development set out in our government's plan. This plan aims to create free healthcare for everyone, high quality education for everyone and employment for everyone." Cheers and ululations rippled through the crowd, the noise swelling.

"On education we can be happy that results from school leavers are improving and the new nurse training college opens next year." More cheers.

"For healthcare, new blood testing equipment is expected from Germany this year and more doctors are expected."

"Not true," a lone voice called. Muttering edged through the crowd.

"Be quiet. Let the comrade speak."

"On housing......."

"What about jobs Michael. We came to hear about jobs."

"Let the man speak. Tell us about the new houses."

The two young men on the veranda next to Michael were prowling and peering into the crowd trying to identify the hecklers.

"On housing," Michael continued through the squeaky loudspeaker, "Comrade President is hopeful that next year will see one hundred new homes here in Mbulu."

"Rubbish. Where? Where will they be built?" One of the young boys from the front, with a stick, pointed to the heckler and gestured to his colleague.

"One hundred new homes, with water and electricity."

"Tell us about jobs Michael. When will the factory open?"

"And, so, to jobs," Michael pressed on with his speech, unaffected by hecklers. "You have all read the reports in the press and seen on TV the reports, many of them untrue, about the suggested site for a new factory south of Mbulu,"

"Did he say untrue? What's untrue?" a woman in the front spoke loudly to her neighbour.

"What is true is that Comrade President has been for many months in discussion with certain Chinese investors about their proposals for this area. Our government has offered many incentives and a deal was agreed that would create many hundreds of jobs. And now today at this eleventh hour we have been told by the Chinese company that they favour Uganda instead. I regret to inform you that they have decided to ignore all our offers and cancel the planned investment in jobs and our local economy. There is nothing our President can do about this but we obviously regret the dishonest negotiations on the part of the Chinese."

The noise from the crowd now grew, peppered with cries of "Shame!" and "Liars" and "This is too bad brother."

At the back of the crowd a drum beat started, there were more ululations and part of the crowd started singing a traditional folk song of the victor and the vanquished. A young boy starting waving madly a large yellow flag and the drummer fell in behind him. Soon an impromptu procession had started led by the young flag waver and the drummer. Most of the crowd stayed to listen to Michael's speech but a sizeable portion of the throng marched around the bus stand, passengers leaning out of stranded buses with jeers and cheers.

"It's important," Michael Zuhura continued, "that no-one should take it upon themselves to seek any sort of vengeance over the Chinese people and other foreigners working here. Comrade Elimu has urged me to remind everyone to stay calm and wait for more announcements. He is still hopeful that some new arrangement can be found. In the meantime, everyone should stay peaceful and lawful and calm."

Innocent was waiting on a bus due to leave for Dar an hour and a half ago. The engine was off and with no shade the bus was too hot even with windows open. But Innocent did not want his old dope smoking boys to see him. He could see his group of pals from the bus. From their exaggerated gestures, their caps turned back to front and one or two stamping and dancing to the rhythm of the drum, Innocent could tell that this excitement was growing. He was not ready to be drawn into it and waited agitatedly for the driver to set off. If they left now they would not be in Dar until long after dark and there was no sign of the driver. As he looked across the road he could see that the crowd that had gathered for Michael Zuhura had thinned, that but the marchers following the drummer had been joined by whistles and more flags and was growing. The line was snaking round the wooden stalls and into the bus stand. As more people joined, the drumming grew in intensity, the whistles joined the rhythm and the marchers kept beat so that the snaking procession of drums, flags, chants, sticks and raised fists became quite quickly a protest with no leader. The chants were for jobs and victory. Michael Zuhura had driven off in his Nissan some time ago.

After the march had passed and moved off towards town, swelling its numbers, the buses started their engines and in a great canopy of dust and amid great swirls of diesel fumes a huge convoy of coaches finally pulled away from the bus stand. Innocent sank back into his seat, knees pressed against the seat in front, and with some determination, closed his eyes to sleep.

The march wound its way from the bus stand down the main highway and stopped in front of the municipal compound and the offices of, amongst other officials, Mr Jin, who, having heard about Zuhura's speech, had given instructions to policemen on duty to be vigilant, only allowing access to those individuals with appointments to meet named officials. The policemen were neither vigilant nor fully understood the instructions and whilst they quizzed two women from the kitchen at length, when the march eventually arrived at the compound gates, the guards confirmed that Mr Jin was in his office and briefly joined the dancing themselves, taking care to be back in their small sentry box before Jin emerged in shirt sleeves in the car park.

"Good morning Mr Jin," one of the crowd called out. All seemed good natured at this stage anyway. "Can you confirm what Michael Zuhura has said – that there will be no cement factory in Mbulu?"

"Gentlemen," Zin tried to sound diplomatic. "These are rumours at this stage. Go home, stay calm and wait for more news. We are doing all we can."

"What about those Chinese workers who have opened a work camp up on the Lindi road? What are they doing there if there is to be no factory?" a faceless voice from the mob called out.

"They have nothing to do with this project. They work for another private company. I'll say again, I need to ask you to clear the car park. The Regional Commissioner is expected shortly and we will need to clear the car park." Jin sensed that the crowd was both well-informed and increasingly restless. He retreated back into the building and called on the Police Commissioner whose office was on the next floor.

The drum beats were becoming louder and more insistent. There were more raised fists, more cries of 'Forward with the people' and a young man swung his stick viciously at a government Landcruiser parked nearby. The windscreen split and shattered. There were thin cheers from the crowd but many ran as a line of twenty or so policemen in formation emerged at a jog from the rear of the building. They stood with rifles aimed at the crowd while the Police Commissioner from a balcony on the first floor shouted through his handheld speaker,

"Disperse now. You will not be warned again. Disperse now or these soldiers will fire."

Most of the crowd had run away on seeing the soldiers and the voice over the loudspeaker silenced the drums. The stomping stopped, arms were lowered and one man emerged from the crowd,

"We are going Commissioner, but can you at least tell us what the government plans to do for us if the Chinese pull out."

"Go home and switch on your radios. Go home now and no-one will be hurt."

The protestor threw down his yellow peaked cap in disgust, stamped on it and turned away.

The Police Commissioner passed the loudspeaker to his aide and barked at the woman sitting outside his office to get the Deputy Minister for Home Affairs on the telephone.

Innocent arrived in the great sprawling bus stand west of Dar just after eight that night. The driver had driven furiously and Innocent at times thought his nerve wouldn't hold. He'd tried to sleep, tried to pray, tried to talk to his neighbour.

He made his way not to Elias or to any of the thieves with whom he'd built a strained friendship. Since Frank's death Innocent had determined to have nothing more to do with them, but he needed a place to stay. Gerold had given him the address of a priest where he said he would be able to stay, at least for a few nights. He asked an old man at a fruit stall for some directions. It was a long way from the bus stand but Innocent was in no hurry. The tall flood lights illuminating the bus stand had the effect of flattening the landscape so that the rutted tracks, the flood drains and the footpaths became one dull amber nightscape unfeeling, unwelcoming but awfully real. Innocent felt a wave of panic wash over him as he felt suddenly utterly alone, but it passed just as quickly and was replaced with a form of relief from the anonymity of being alone in such a huge city. He had a long way to walk and keeping his eye on landmarks such as an office block, a football stadium and a hotel he made his way slowly across town to the church of St Anne.

When he arrived at the church in the early hours of the morning, the gates to the compound were locked. The night-watchman spoke to him through the wire fence,

"What do you want, brother? It's late. Everyone is in bed."

"Father Gerold has sent me. Father Sixtus is expecting me."

"Father Sixtus is away but you can sleep in here if you have nowhere." He pointed to the wooden shed which served as his guard's station, living quarters and bedroom.

"Thank you. What is your name?"

"Matthew. And you?"

"I'm Innocent. I have nowhere. I'm from Mbulu. Father Gerold sent me here." A mattress lay in one corner and Innocent was directed by Matthew to sleep there.

"Don't worry about me. I'll be on duty here and I can make a comfortable place with those bags." He pointed to some used plastic rice sacks. Innocent made himself comfortable for the night and the following morning introduced himself to Sixtus. Matthew took him to Sixtus as he was eating breakfast, a hard-boiled egg and some cold rice. He was a man in his fifties, perhaps older, round and short and with a shine to his complexion that was only dulled by the grey that gave a dull furry haze to part of it. He wore silver-rimmed spectacles that caused him to peer as he looked at you.

"You're welcome. Gerold sent me a message but I didn't know when to expect you. What will you do here?"

"I'm not sure yet Father. I'm pleased to be able to help you in any way you think best."

"But do you not have family back in Mbulu? What are your plans?"

Innocent hesitated, not knowing whether to lie or not.

"No matter," Sixtus continued. "You will do what you will do. Eat some breakfast and then ask Matthew what you should do. I'm sure he has plenty of work for you. Is that right Matthew?"

Matthew was making tea in a small scullery to the back of the room where they sat.

"Leave him with me Father. He will be fine with me."

As Sixtus left, Innocent sat at the table and helped himself to eggs and rice.

There was a warmth to the natural welcome here that

had immediately smoothed Innocent's anxieties and Innocent set about a day's chores with Matthew with energy. There was cleaning to do, there were errands at the shops, and washing of clothes. Most complicated but also most interesting was the repair of Sixtus' old car. It needed a puncture repairing and Matthew said that it would need to go to the mechanic. Could he drive? No? The mechanic would have to collect it but he should go with the car in order to be able to report accurately what needed doing.

A young man in blue overalls arrived and Innocent watched as he first of all changed the tyre then sat in the driver's seat and called Innocent to go with him. They drove a few blocks to a block built hut and some wooden sheds. Outside, stood a couple of old pick-ups that had obviously been in serious smashes and a couple of saloon cars. A youngish boy, perhaps fifteen, was wielding a huge steel bar and attempting to prise a tyre off its wheel. The mechanic opened the back door of Sixtus' car and called on the young boy to take the wheel and fix its puncture. Innocent watched intently as the mechanic started removing first a pipe, then a metal box, then some tubing, then spark plugs and so it went on until the floor around the car seemed to be covered with screws and bolts and bits of metal. Innocent had no idea how anyone could possibly remember how it all went back together again. After a couple of hours, Innocent was assisting the mechanic, passing this tool, handing that piece of the engine. They exchanged some easy pleasantries and Innocent felt quite at home, they left their work to go a container shop some fifty meters down the road and took tea. The mechanic, Godfrey, had chapatti with his tea but Innocent declined.

"What's your business then, Innocent?" Godfrey went straight to the point and took Innocent off his guard.

"I am looking for work. Do you know anyone who needs a hand?"

Later that morning, Innocent walked back to the church.

"The mechanic says it will not be ready until tomorrow at the earliest," Innocent reported to Matthew.

"No matter," said Matthew, cleaning two brass candlesticks. "You can go back tomorrow and check that he's working on it. If you leave him we will not hear from him for weeks. Africans are so lazy, but I suppose you know that already."

That evening, Sixtus, Matthew and Innocent ate together. Matthew invited Innocent to start by leading them in prayer before the meal. Innocent stumbled and hesitated. He knew no words and felt embarrassed and inadequate. Matthew took over,

"Bless us, O Lord, for these your gifts which we are about to receive through your kindness, through Christ our Lord."

"Amen," said Sixtus, who had already lifted his knife and fork. After supper, as Matthew and Innocent dried the dishes and put them away, Matthew returned to the matter of prayers,

"For tomorrow, I want you to learn those prayers so that you can take a full part in the life of this house. We pray each day and you must be part of it."

Matthew had given Innocent a small room in the back of the house. It had a bed and a chair, a metal grill for a window and one light bulb but no shade. That night as Innocent lay in bed trying to memorise prayers before and after food, his mind turned to Mbulu and Rose. What was she thinking? What would she tell Babu Jackson or her mother? Why was he lying in a single bed in a mission house in Dar? Matthew and Sixtus were kind people but they must know that this is not his home. A now familiar panic started to rise in him. It started somewhere above his stomach and lying prone as he was, soon started to suffocate him. He sat upright and breathed deeply. He stood at the metal grill and leaned out to try and fill his lungs more quickly. He threw himself back down on his bed. He was worthless. He was nothing to Rose, his friends meant nothing to him, everything he'd ever tried had failed, or worse. He'd done wicked things for which he could never be forgiven. Forgiven? He could not even maintain his faith in Jesus Christ. If God existed, Innocent was sure to be damned. Finally, exhaustion came like a cool breeze. He slept and woke early, eager to start his daily activities with Matthew. Mornings came as a hard-earned treat.

After his breakfast of vegetable broth made from last night's supper, Innocent cleaned the church and then was sent to the market, a seething mass of stalls and small shops. He was to buy a number of basic provisions - oil, rice and flour. He asked each shop-holder if they had work. At a small mobile phone shop, he impressed the young owner with his knowledge of the latest phones and their functions. Hesitantly the shop-owner, Rafi, agreed to let Innocent stay and serve customers. He'd give him a day's trial and see how that went. The work was easy and Innocent felt at ease with the young people asking questions to which he always had an easy answer.

But nightfall came like a blanket muffling any good spirit he might have nurtured that day. After supper and prayers, Matthew and Sixtus left him alone. He wanted to ask Matthew to stay but knew that such a request would be unwelcome and he returned to his small room, peering out of the steel grill, watching the old dog that slept out there and waiting for sleep, hoping that the night would for him, for once, be peaceful.

Chapter Thirteen

There had been smoke in the skies for several days, but today it was much closer and now the rumours of fighting came with the names of villages and people. Lukanga had been hit last week and this week the fighting was approaching Mbulu. Since the announcement by the Chinese that there would be no factory and no new jobs created, fighting and stone throwing seemed to start without warning. It could happen anywhere at any time.

Two days ago, some Chinese workers living in their compound out of town had been attacked, one man had been killed with a machete and two others badly hurt. Their co-workers had run to their defence and the local attackers had run to hide in the bush. The following day a larger group of young Africans had approached the compound and were driven back by two army vehicles full of soldiers. Rumours were everywhere of resistance to government attacks, of objections to government corruption and revenge attacks on local Chinese still working in the area. For some reason, amidst all these rumours, came the reality of attacks on priests and calls for Muslims to support their brothers in *jihad*. Young men with fierce unfeeling eyes shouted at women to cover themselves; they called on the village elders to support their call for a general strike.

"Shut up your shops! Close your businesses. Show the

government we are serious."
Everyone cheered, but inside they were either frightened or weary. Young boys cheered and threw stones at passing cars, but older men shook their heads and sighed. They knew how this would end. They had seen this before. It started with alarming radio broadcasts. Neighbours stooped and crouched around the tiny radio in Jimmy's, 'New Cutz' hairdressers.

Rose wrapped Noah to her back in a kanga and hurried to her sister's house. Jacline lived with her husband's family in another part of town, a brisk walk of perhaps thirty minutes. Anna stayed behind to watch their home and phoned to check that their small shop was closed and shuttered.

The walk to Anna's took her past the short line of new shops. There were five shops, built some years ago with cement blocks and now were always called 'Five New Shops'. Each shop was sealed shut with steel shutters but one, Mr Ally's electrical spares shop, still had rolls of cable, fans, and one or two hi-fi systems sitting on the porch outside the shop. Mr Ally was inside carrying boxes of electrical parts into the steel container at the rear of his shop. A group of young boys had gathered on the cement pavement outside his shop and were shouting his name,
"Mr Ally, old man. Come out here."
His faint voice from inside could be heard from the cavernous depths of boxes and shelves.

"I'm coming. Please wait one minute."

A young man, older than the others, dressed in white with a distinctive white *kufi* arrived and spoke harshly to the group,
"Where is he? Bring him out."
Two of the group ran in; the others waited, listening to the shouts and bangs of boxes falling and tinkling of broken glass, until they emerged a moment later with the small grey Mr Ally between them. Mr Ally was small and thin and wore grey trousers tied at the waist with a thick brown belt. Both trousers and belt had been made for someone else, for a much larger man.
"Old man. Did you not hear our call for solidarity?"
"I was just packing some things away. Please give me a moment."
"But all your neighbours have closed their shops. Why is yours open?"
Mr Ally looked down and shook his head. The scene froze for a moment, no-one moving, then the angry young man in pristine white *kufi* raised his head, arched his eyebrows and lifted his chin towards the shop.
"Go boys. Show him what we do to cowards and traitors."
And with that one boy raised a leg and kicked one of the stand fans off the *baraza*. Its legs broke as it tumbled into the dirty street. The others quickly joined the destruction, using sticks or *panga* to smash everything they could reach. While they did this their

leader took a cigarette lighter from inside his *kameez*, bent to collect some papers from the front of the shop and carefully lit a small fire with a cardboard box. Slowly and deliberately, delicately, he tended the small fire until the box was fully alight and he could direct the others to bring out Mr Ally's wares and burn them in front of him. Mr Ally, held by the arms by one larger boy, watched and shook his head.

In the distance, a woman could be heard screaming as she ran towards the burning shop.

"Stop! Please stop!"

Rose recognised her immediately as Mr Ally's wife, Asha. Rose ran to intercept her. Asha brushed her aside and ran up to the young man in white.

"Are you not ashamed of yourself. This is everything we own."

"Don't speak to me like that," he said, placing his face close to Asha. "He is a greedy old man. He should think of others."

With that, he brushed past her and walked away. As he did so, gunfire rang out; the clear deep-bellied rattle of a machine gun. Young boys, still dragging boxes of cable, plugs, screws and even a TV out of the shop, stopped, looked, then ran. They ran away from the gunfire and in the direction of Rose's house. The man in white continued walking. Further down the track, from round a bend where the shops peter out and smaller houses began, appeared a group of soldiers, perhaps six in total. They wore stiff khaki uniforms, high-legged boots with a deep polish and red berets. Each of them, but one, carried a rifle, slung casually over their shoulder or dripping from their hands. Only one carried a smaller machine gun, held purposefully in front of him, pointed now, directly at Rose.

Rose could turn and run but she was sure they would chase her and that could make things worse. She decided to stand her ground and brave it out. Two of them stopped her.

"What's the hurry, sister?"

Rose stood still, but said nothing. These soldiers were not much older than her. Young men had left Mbulu to join the army. For young men who failed their exams, the army was a good job, a steady salary, good food and a pension. These soldiers were not from here, though. They were not her tribe. They showed her no respect. One of them, the taller one, went to stroke her face with the back of his hand; she flinched, but stood her ground. The other walked casually around her, grinning, pointing, then went to remove Noah from the kanga on her back. Noah was silent but his back went rigid and Rose ducked to avoid the soldier's arms. He grabbed her and the other taller one put down his gun. Rose screamed, but having stood up, he began to unpick the knot tying the kanga while the soldier at Rose's back held baby Noah.

"If you run, we'll just kill the little one." Rose was about to scream but no sound came. She froze. Noah was placed roughly on the ground,

"Stay there little one. Don't move."

The two soldiers then moved around Rose and backed her towards a small alley between two houses. The alley was narrow, shaded and stank of urine. Two hens pecked at some rubbish on the ground. Noah found a plastic bottle top in the dirt near him, picked it up, shook it in his fist and popped it in his mouth.

"Leave her!" A voice from across the street rang out and the soldiers reacted with a nervous glance over their shoulders. Further down the street the other soldiers had stopped the young man in white. One of the soldiers had knocked his hat from his head and was prodding him with his rifle. The young man ran. He ran towards the baby sitting in the dirt but, there, two soldiers were emerging from a passageway and so he ran towards the shop on the other side of the street. A path next to that shop led into a small field of maize. The soldiers chased; there was a gunshot; men were shouting; Mrs Ally shouted,

"No!"

Mrs Ally ran into the field of maize, short green plants in neat lines along a shallow furrow; her feet pressed into the soft earth and she tripped as her sandal slid from under her and she stooped to remove her sandals, the faster to run. Ahead of her, the soldiers had stopped and were talking, one of them laughed, another patted him on his shoulder, hands slapped in high-fives.

As she got closer, she could see the body of the young man in white strewn awkwardly across the furrows, his legs twisted at an impossible angle. She stopped when she saw the dark red patch staining the bright white *kameez*; she peered until she saw the muddy mess at the back of his head; then she turned and ran. Rose didn't run. She heard the shot and screamed.

"Noah. My baby"

She stood, winced, tied her kanga and ran out of the alley. She ran and swept up Noah in her arms without breaking her step. She pressed the little one to her face, squeezing his podgy limbs to her flesh – first his face then his belly, and his legs, smothering him with her face, smelling each patch of flesh, assuring herself that he was unharmed. Noah stood up in his mother's arms and waved a small clenched fist in which he clenched a blue plastic bottle top.

Mrs Ally ran towards Rose

"Come with me Rose. We have to tell Tamba."

"I have to get to my sister and warn her. I have tried to call her but there is no signal."

Village elders had warned the community previously that this time would come and when it did, the Authorities were likely to block phone networks, stopping people locally from organising themselves, minimising resistance. Consequently, the soldiers who they had just encountered, arrived almost without warning. They were peacekeepers, sent by the government to protect businesses, but everyone knew them to be thugs who would molest your children and steal your things. Rose had heard the other day of two soldiers arriving at a house in another village and demanding, at gunpoint, that they give them their television. They strapped it to a motorcycle and took it away.

"We'll walk as far as the big shops together. You might be able to pick up a piki-piki there. I'll go and see Tamba. He must know. And he must tell us what to do."

"Are you not worried about Mr Ally? Will he be safe?"

"I think they've done their worst for now. He will be OK"

As they talked they walked; they stepped passed a large pile of smouldering tyres, giving off a black acrid smoke – the rusted and twisted mesh from the tyre garishly exposed; trees, roughly cut and dragged from the roadside lined their way; occasionally they had to step over these makeshift road blocks and could see where smaller fires had been built to cook maize and keep young men warm. The army vehicles had then barged these flimsy remains back to the road edge. But the roads were empty. No children played in the street; no girls sat on their *baraza*.

Mrs Ally was right. There were one or two boys with motorcycles under a flame tree at the big market. They leaned against their bikes. One of them smoked a cigarette. As Rose approached one of them raised his hand, the palm face up, a gesture to say, "Hire me." Rose told one of them the district, the other boy clicked his tongue as she wrapped her kanga and then slid deftly on to the seat. The young boy positioned his dark glasses and set off in a small burst of dust and smoke. Rose rested one hand on the boy's shoulder. They drove through the narrow streets and alleys weaving an intricate path from the market to her sister's home near the edge of town.

Her sister's family had bought land outside the town some years ago. The grandfather would bring out the creased and slightly grubby paperwork at the slightest opportunity whenever visitors sat with him to greet him. Now they lived in a half-built house made of cement blocks, occupying two small rooms but which were accessed through a large twisted wooden door opening into a small courtyard off which were entrances to as yet unbuilt rooms. In the courtyard, an old woman leaned with a large plastic bowl at her feet over a pile of wet washing; she picked each brightly coloured item and rubbed the cloth roughly in her hands before pounding it back into the water then dragging it out to squeeze and wring it. Finally, she stretched it roughly and hoisted it over a washing line strung between two sections of unfinished wall.

"Hodi, hodi," Rose called as she stepped into the courtyard.

"Karibu", called the old woman without looking away from her washing.

It was clear that whatever her sister's family was doing, the unrest in town and the violence of the soldiers had not affected this family yet. A young woman dressed in a long black shawl covering her head and wrapped tightly round her head came out from the small room. The two sisters greeted one another with the slightest of kisses as they turned and entered the house. The doorway gave way to a dark hallway off which was a stuffy shaded room, garishly coloured curtains strung at the window with rusty nails. A small child sat on the floor, trying to crawl but as yet unable to shuffle more than a few inches before flailing arms required his mother to pick him up. Rose's sister held the baby in her arms and sliding a hand inside her shawl, offered her breast to the baby. He sucked eagerly.

"How is it? Have you not heard the gunfire?"

"Yes, of course. But I haven't been into town. How is mother?"

Rose's sister and her mother spoke rarely, their mother relying on Rose to serve as mutual messenger for any important news.

"She's fine. Ally's shop was destroyed just now and then they shot one of the young militants. I couldn't see who it was."

"Why do you call them that Rose? Abdul tells me they are fighting for our future. The government calls them militants because they are worried that we will support them."

Rose sighed derisively and waved her hand.

"Jacline, call them soldiers, militants, whatever you call them, they are killing people and hurting our lives. I just wish it would stop."

"You have to pick a side. And you must never support these criminals calling themselves soldiers."
An awkward silence bridged the gap between them. It was a sisterly silence, but it left spaces that only fear and resentment would fill.
"I've come just to see that you are all fine. Our phones don't work and travelling is dangerous."
"We are fine," sighed Jacline and, after a while, "Thanks, sister, for coming. You have blessed us."

The soldiers left eventually. They stayed in town for some weeks. They bashed down doors, smacked old men in their faces, broke some furniture, drank cheap alcohol and sat with their feet up in other people's chairs, smoking Mr Ally's cigarettes. But after some weeks they left. Rumours flickered like dying flames in an old fire; rumours that the soldiers were coming back next week or next month; rumours that the government had ordered a crackdown and that compensation would be paid to those whose businesses had been harmed; rumours that everyone was to be given a small piece of land. But these rumours faded as quickly as they came and soon the village returned to the peaceful poverty that it had once known for as many generations as anyone could remember.

Chapter Fourteen

Rose woke to the sound of rain hammering on the new roof. She felt immensely proud that her home was now dry and so very, very loud. When it rained like this, all talk had to stop. The children could cry and Innocent might shout and slam but it would all be silenced by the beautiful din of rain hammering on a shiny new tin roof.

She leapt up, grabbed a cloth kanga, and ran out to place plastic buckets to catch water from the roof.
"Come here, my precious and see the rain. See how it bounces in the bucket." She swept the baby up in her arm. She would wait and watch the rain before starting her day. She still needed to light a fire to make porridge. She needed to buy flour and oil and if her neighbour would pay her for the soap she gave her last week she could afford some kerosene for the lamp. Later, she would take the hoe and scrape the red soil, ready for planting a few seeds for this year's maize. This early rain meant it was already time.
Anna came to the house as soon as the rain eased.
"Rose! Rose! Bring those buckets in." Rose was sitting sifting rice.
"We should try and buy a new bigger bin soon. I saw them at Lucas' place the other day. They can now store a lot of good water in those big bins."
"Well, Mama, there are many things we need to buy before we buy one. I would like to buy solar panels."
"Solar? Nonsense. If you can't afford a bucket to keep

water, you won't be buying solar panels."

Rose had a good idea exactly how much Innocent would give her – not every week, but every few days. Sometimes she had to shout; sometimes she had to sulk, but in the end, he would hand over a few thousand shillings. Rose was good at keeping a check on what they needed and what they spent each week. Innocent had had great plans for their small shamba, had sworn that they would grow maize and cassava and bananas. Those plans had come to nothing and Rose had now become accustomed to living on her wage and whatever Babu or her mother offered. Rose knew she had to make her own way and not rely on him. In truth, she'd never relied on him. She'd just loved the look and the feel of him.

It was not a happy start. Innocent had never been open about his life in Dar. Rose had never been to the city, never asked and never been told just what he did or who he saw when he went there. And he travelled to Dar often. At first every other month, then every few weeks and nowadays she assumed he was there all the time as he was rarely at home. A darker side had shown itself in recent months, or at least a side of Innocent she failed utterly to understand. Before he'd left last time, he'd spent days sleeping. He'd not been to the bus stand – he rarely saw anyone when he came home and when anyone asked about him, told Rose brusquely to say that he wasn't well or that he was busy. When they were alone, he played with Noah.

On more than once occasion he made him a small truck from a plastic bottle and four bottle tops for wheels. Noah was too small to understand but enjoyed waddling and toddling, trying to grab the bottle from Innocent's hands. It seemed to Rose that only on occasions like this was Innocent truly happy. With adults, especially Anna or Babu, he was surly, often rude and usually silent.

"Well?" Her mother wouldn't let it drop. Rose was Anna's favourite daughter and her biggest disappointment. She was also the most likely to care for her when she became frail.

Rose ignored her. She was confident nowadays in her friendship with her mother. There was a time that she had needed her. Her mother borrowed the money to build a house. She had spoken to Innocent's family about a bride price. She had showed Rose all manner of simple domestic activities that helped her to keep her small house clean. She showed her what she should do to make sure that food was ready when it was needed. She gave her a large pan in which Rose could make chapatti and fry small doughy buns to make a few shillings each morning. Rose was young but she was growing up quickly.

Once her baby was born, Rose quickly realised that many of the ambitions she held as a schoolgirl, the hopes and expectations that she had then were shallow. When first she realised that she was carrying

Innocent's baby, she felt angry and scared – angry at the wasted opportunity he had surely caused; and scared at what her life now would be like. Before Noah, her life had been mapped in her mind as a simple series of tests to pass – school – college – work – and mixed in there somewhere were the blurred and shadowy pictures of a man, a baby, a house, her mother. Now, there was no plan, just the immediate needs of today, tomorrow and next week. Thoughts of next year were hazy. When she tried to pin down her misty ideas into a plan with dates and figures and people they sped off into the distance and she found herself daydreaming about some detail such as what dress she might wear or if she had a good harvest from her maize. It was as though the act of giving birth had switched something in her head that meant that plans for the future, as an innate defence mechanism, would never be too serious and then could never disappoint.

Rose was sweeping her porch, bent double with a besom, one hand bent behind her, resting on the base of her back. She heard screams and shouting which must have been from the end of the track where the next cluster of mud houses sat close to three large mango trees. She dropped the besom, slung the baby on her hip and walked then ran to the end of the track. The screams were not the usual noises – a child being admonished or a fight between man and wife – these were more serious. A group of women had gathered at the end of her track. One of this group was gesticulating and the commotion from this huddle was growing. Children skipped around the group, some stood on tiptoes, craning to see the woman at the centre of the group. She was wailing and beating her forehead with her hands as she cried.

Rose straightened, still holding her back and leaned backwards, the pleasure of stretching brought a frown to her forehead but her gaze was still directed towards the group making such a noise. It grew quickly to number perhaps fifty people, one or two older women scurrying from their homes to learn more. Rose's mother, Anna, approached the group with some authority and parted some of the women at the edge of the gathering; as she did so, others turned and made way for her. Rose took a few steps down the track towards the crowd, the better to hear what her mother might have to say.

"What is the matter, mother? What's happened?"

The woman looked and with a wide swoop of her arms flung herself at Anna. Her cries grew louder, hysterical as Anna struggled to have both of them stand. After some moments, a dirty plastic chair was lifted over the heads of the crowd and the woman was urged to sit. Anna leaned into her face

"Tell me Amina. Stop crying and tell me."

The woman's cries had turned to sobs but she could not speak.

"It's her child. He is dead"

"Is this true Amina? Your boy is dead?"

Amina looked up, her mouth opened but no words

came out and then came a great bellow which started somewhere behind her but grew to a full-throated scream, not shrill but persistent.

"A snake bit him and when they found him he was already dead," said someone in the crowd.

"Where is he now?"

"His father has him."

As Amina's cried ebbed to sobs, so the crowd thinned. After some minutes, Anna guided Amina back to Rose's house, a young boy was enlisted to carry the chair and Amina drawn to sit on Rose's porch and take a damp cloth to her face.

As they sat, the three of them said little while Noah played with an empty plastic bottle. Rose occasionally adjusted her headscarf and picked at her hair, but for the most part they sat in silence. In the distance, a plume of smoke rose into the sky, a thin line at first, then opening to become a dark cloud then paled to a grey smudge as the wind caught it and took it away.

Chapter Fifteen

Mbulu had grown accustomed to the presence of soldiers around town. They leaned against shops near the municipal offices, they slung their machine guns around their shoulders like duffel bags, smoking with boys at the bus stand and flirting with women at the market. Few trusted them, though. Not one of them was from Mbulu. The army was very professional at ensuring no soldiers serving in 'peace-keeping' in Mbulu were from that town or surrounding area. The army needed to know where its soldiers' loyalties lay. And the people of Mbulu knew it too. For all the flirting and joshing and leaning on motorcycles no-one was in any doubt that these soldiers could and would point their guns on them when called upon to do so. And they didn't need much provocation.

Innocent noticed the jeeps and the personnel carriers from the bus as he approached the town. Each of the small villages lining the main highway to Mbulu had two or three soldiers posted. Sometimes they stood by the bus stand; in others, they stood near the small wooden shack with its thatched roof covering a blistered pool table; in others, they sat alone under the shade of a tree, village elders looking on. Village life chattered and hummed along around them, as though these soldiers weren't there. But like a fresh scab that left alone will eventually dry and fall away, if picked it will become again raw and sometimes bleed.

Innocent pressed his face against the glass to get a better view as the coach pulled away. As the bus approached the larger buildings of Mbulu – the new glass fronted bank, the regional headquarters of the national training agency, the District Commissioner's residence – the military presence was more formal and more obvious. Soldiers at these 'strategic' centres were more numerous and there was definitely no lounging. They stood to attention and stopped local cars at random to ask for papers, demanding who was going where and why.

Innocent made his way out of town, past the primary school, along the dusty tracks to the small collection of houses where Anna lived. He would need to pass those houses to reach his own place. Hopefully Rose and Noah were alone and he could arrive quietly and there would be fewer questions. As he passed the small hamlet where Rose had grown up he noticed that more building work was underway and more land was under cultivation. The maize fields now reached as far as the mbuyu trees in the distance and towards the hill on which his house sat alone, someone had started clearing the scrub ready for cultivation.

Rose and the baby were not at the house. The door was not locked so he knew that she would not be far away and saw in the distance the bent figure at the top of the hill. She was swinging the hoe in a short raking movement and he approached saw that Noah was strapped to her back. She was raking stones and weeds out of the ground in readiness for sowing. She stopped as he approached but said nothing.

"How have you been?" he asked at last.

"We're fine. How long will you stay this time?" She knew it was not what he wanted to hear but she couldn't hold back.

"I'm home. And I want to stay if I can."

"This is your home. What can I say?"

"Where's the young girl?"

"She is visiting her family. Babu gave her the bus fare. She'll be back in a few days." She passed the hoe to him and made her way down the field. He waited and after a few yards, she looked over her shoulder. "This one needs to eat and then sleep."

Rose had fallen into a comfortable daily routine without Innocent. She would rise early, feed Noah and take him to her mother. When the young girl was there, Rose could leave Noah confidently with her as she went to work in the college. With help from her mother she earned enough to buy food and fuel and her grandfather was always on hand if needed. She did not like asking him. As time passed and she had time to watch him and Anna, she noticed the tension between them.

As a young girl, she'd always been happy to be the reason for Babu's smile, the object of his attentions and his small treats, but now, as she fell into life as a mother, she noticed more and more the unkindnesses that he visited on Anna. Perhaps he didn't realise it and Anna had seemingly grown so accustomed that she barely winced at all, but the cruelty was there. Rose had never been treated like that and she felt more and more for her mother.

Jackson came to visit that evening. If he was surprised to see Innocent he did not say so, barely acknowledging him, but instead sitting down to tell Rose news of the day's developments.

"The DC is getting more worried by the day. Each day there is news of attacks on shops, mostly non-Muslim shops and the soldiers do nothing."

The three of them sat under the eerie light of a small kerosene lamp.

"Father Gerold has been told by the bishop to pay for a guard at his house."

"How will this problem be solved, Babu?"

"They must start preaching tolerance in the mosques and the government must make some public concessions to show that Muslims are being given recognition."

"What does that mean?" Innocent felt the need to participate. Jackson looked at him but turned to Rose to answer the question.

"They feel that all the senior positions are filled by Christians and that they are disadvantaged. This latest decision to cancel the cement factory contract is being used by hard-line Muslims to fuel prejudice and allow them to tell ordinary people here in Mbulu that if the majority in this town were Christian then the jobs would still be coming."

"That's nonsense," said Rose. "This government is corrupt and inefficient. It's got nothing to do with Muslims or Christians. That's a convenient excuse for some."

As Jackson set off home, the flares of explosions followed by cracks that sounded like thunder but which everyone knew to be bullets, made him hurry his pace. Innocent lay next to Rose that night, still. He was relieved to be home. He no longer lay awake waiting for panic to take over; instead he listened for the crack of bullets or the boom of a home-made explosion.

Innocent woke before Rose and went to the field to complete the work which she had left unfinished. By the time she emerged from the house the field was ready for sowing. Innocent felt pleased but would not risk waiting for words of thanks or compliments. Instead, he returned the hoe, washed himself and made his way over to the church and his old friend Father Gerold.

The track to the church crossed one of the main roads to the bus stand and the market. Some men had built a barrier using a young tree and two steel drums. They had placed piles of sticks across the road and a pile of rocks at each side. Two or three machetes lay in a heap on one pile of stones. As Innocent crossed the road to continue along the track – a shortcut for those on foot or bicycle – the young men, some wearing cloths wound round their heads in the way of bandana, looked at him, did not smile nor greet him, but watched him as they continued their conversation. Innocent continued on his way to church where Father Gerold was working in his house, trying to write notes at his table.

"Good morning Innocent. It does me good to see you back home. How are you? How is Dar? Sixtus tells me you have made a second home there."

"Sixtus and Matthew are very kind. But I want to live here in Mbulu, Father. I just sometimes seem to need to be away." Gerold nodded. They sat together for a few minutes, each thinking their own thoughts.

"I'm preparing Sunday's homily and I have jobs for you if you have time."

"Of course. Just say. What is this I hear about a guard for the church? Is it true?"

"It's true that the bishop has told me to pay for one. It's not true that he has given me any money to do so. So, for the time being, there will be no guard."

"I heard gunshots last night. And these young men at the barriers, not all from here, look like they're preparing for a fight. What do they hope to stop?"

"They are stopping cars. I don't know why. That barrier will be down before evening. The soldiers will come and remove it. It happens every day."

The soldiers did remove it that evening. Two soldiers dragged the tree and the drums to the side of the road while two more soldiers held their guns ready pointed at the youths who had gathered – twenty or more by the time the soldiers had finished. The soldiers backed away to their jeep and fired one warning shot to the sky. One or two younger boys ran but the older ones, facing the soldiers jeered. The soldiers drove away at speed.

Innocent, sitting in Gerold's room, wanted to understand more.

"My homily," explained Gerold. "will call on everyone to reject the hatred being peddled by a tiny minority. The government does not have the solution because it cannot create jobs without international donors. The solution to Mbulu's problems lies with the people of Mbulu. If we allow some hotheads who will abuse the name of Islam to divide us then we should expect trouble."

"From what I've seen, those hotheads will not want to be called hotheads and they will not be turned from their course."

"You are right, up to a point. And the soldiers are making matters worse at the moment. The more violent the soldiers, the more likely those young militants will respond with violence. They know they can achieve more by killing us, the people, than by attacking the soldiers."

"Killing? You think there will be killings?"

"I think that these two sides will not stop before people are killed."

"Ah. That hurts me Father. What is the solution?"

"That I don't know. And the weak human being that I

am, I don't propose a solution in my homily other than prayer and tolerance."

"Prayer and tolerance. You are right."

"Words are cheap, Innocent. Honestly. I'm as worried as you."

They were silent. Gerold deep in thought about his Sunday sermon; Innocent not fearful, but anxious to do something worthwhile.

"I will be your guard tonight, Father. I'll stay here with you. It will be better."

"No. That's very kind but you must go to Rose and your child."

"I'm not needed there, Father. Rose manages well without me. It's better that I'm here."

Gerold sighed. Innocent cleared Gerold's supper things and after some minutes in the kitchen, came back and said goodnight. He got up closed the door behind him and gathered some cloths and some sacks with which to make a bed in the porch of the church. He walked round the church and noted that the second gate to the compound at the back of the church, looking on to scrub, was locked. On the way round, he snapped a good branch from a young tree and peeled off smaller branches to fashion what he could use as a stick. He sat upright in the porch, the stick between his legs and waited for Gerold to switch off his light. He leaned back and lay, eyes wide open, listening.

The night was noisier than the previous night and at

the church he was much closer to town than he was at home. He thought it best that at least Rose and Noah were some way from the trouble and safer. The night was warm. Mosquitoes bit him often. He lit a cigarette, then a small fire from sticks and leaves. The smoke filled the porch and made him cough so he stood to walk around the compound. Sound seemed to travel more easily in the dark and at the wire fence surrounding the church grounds he could hear men's voices quite clearly. He couldn't hear well enough to understand, but he could tell hear voices raised, calling out, then three gunshots in quick succession, then silence. Innocent stood still, craning to hear more, but the men's voices were replaced with dogs barking. He paced the length of the perimeter fence again and again until he grew tired. When he finally returned to the makeshift bed in the porch, he had slept for less than an hour before it was dawn, Gerold was awake and noises from within the house caused to Innocent to get up.

It was Saturday and Mbulu would see offices closed but the market busy. Innocent borrowed Gerold's old bicycle to go the market. Gerold needed some provisions and had asked Innocent to look for a small radio. He took the longer route up the busy main road where some smaller electrical shops might have the small radio Gerold wanted. He stopped to ask at two shops but the radios were either too expensive or far too big. As he continued up the hill towards the market, the effects of the soldiers' presence and the daily tensions with young extremists was obvious. He passed four army jeeps and twenty or soldiers spaced at intervals patrolling the length of this road. A makeshift barrier close to the market had been pulled away from the road. Porches, baraza or veranda would normally see women sitting on the floor whilst sisters, mothers or friends would painstakingly plait their hair in readiness for a family wedding or some other Saturday night festivity. Today, the fronts of people's houses were vacant. Two children played football in a side street; their names were called and they ran inside.

The market at least seemed normal and Innocent could buy the fish and rice easily. Innocent had left his bicycle at Mkonga's hardware shop – Mkonga would watch it for him. When he returned, the shop was surrounded by a group of four soldiers. They had a young Muslim boy against the wall. One soldier prodded him with his finger. Before Innocent could take his bicycle a large crowd of men and women had gathered in the open space in front of Mkonga's shop. Innocent moved to the edge of the square and watched. One soldier turned to see with some alarm the size of the crowd that had gathered so quickly. He nudged his colleague and the four soldiers turned to face the crowd. A stone was thrown and one soldier fired into the sky. The crowd stood and slowly moved forward. Some youths had climbed on to the veranda from the opposite side and were edging towards Mkonga's shop from the other end. Blaring horns and a man's voice over a loudspeaker broke the tension. The voice shouted for the crowd to disperse and the jeep drove at speed towards the crowd. People ran out of the way to avoid being hit by the jeep which braked in a cloud of dust in front of Mkonga's shop. The four soldiers quickly jumped off the veranda and up into the rear of the jeep. The jeep reversed, spilling people from the crowd to either side as it made its way out of the market.

Innocent's return journey was more difficult. The soldiers had now placed the makeshift barricade in the road and were using it themselves to stop people and traffic and questioning everyone. Four or five youths were being held at gunpoint in the back of the jeep. Two older men were berating the soldiers
"Let them go, you thugs. They've done nothing." The soldiers ignored them but one boy in the jeep was hit on his back with a stick. It angered the old men and they shouted again,
"If this continues, there will be trouble. Perhaps that's what you thugs want."

Innocent retraced his route and took a series of small tracks behind the shops and houses and in a very long and circuitous way found his way back to Gerold and the church. He had had to change his route several times as more and more soldiers and jeeps and personnel carriers appeared. One half of town was being divided from the other by a line of barricades blocking each of the roads and tracks up to the bus stand and the market. Innocent left the shopping and the bicycle with Gerold and immediately ran to his home and Rose and Noah.

Innocent ran the kilometre and a half down tracks and little marked paths through shrub. When he arrived at his home Rose and Noah were not there. He made his way to Anna's house, thinking that she might be there. Anna was at home but simply told him that she had not seen Rose or the baby. She shouted after him to go to Babu Jackson's house. Babu Jackson lived in a small rented house on the north side of town, behind the bus stand. To go there, Innocent would have to make his way again through the back streets avoiding soldiers and their barricades and there was no certainty that Rose would be there when he got there. He took a track which would lead him along the edge of town, eventually meeting the main road from the north from where he could make his way towards Babu Jackson and avoid soldiers. It was a long way and would take him over an hour, even running.

After running for ten minutes, he stopped for breath. He reconsidered the idea of making his way to Babu Jackson. If they were not there it would be wasted and it might be better to go back to Gerold, use his mobile phone and try and get hold of Jackson's friends and neighbours for news of Rose and Noah. This seemed a much better idea and he turned and walked back to Gerold and the church. It was almost four o'clock when he arrived at the church. Gerold was talking with some older parishioners on the steps of his house.

"Yes. I have a guard. Here he is. Innocent has agreed to be my guard." The assembled people turned to look at Innocent as he made his way through the gate. One man scoffed,

"He's not reliable. He has no rifle – not even a stick. What protection will he be?"

Another man said, "I have heard reports from Ngugu that the priest there has been threatened. An explosive was thrown at the church and the priest has left for Dar."

"Explosives?", an elderly woman asked, fear obvious in her voice.

"These young Muslims are using the dynamite that the fishermen use to make blasts in the sea and kill fish. They are making bombs in their homes."

"How do you know this?" Gerold tried for calm.

"I know because they are forcing my neighbour to store them in his house. He is too frightened to tell the authorities."

Innocent left the discussion to go inside, to a small room at the back of the house where he lay down and waited for the panic to subside.

Hours later, the house was quiet but in the distance, in Mbulu, Innocent could hear the explosions, the gunfire and occasionally men shouting and some screams. He walked around the compound watching the nightscape light up with flashes followed by thunder claps as explosions ripped the black night open. He did not feel fear; he felt isolation. These horrific scenes were not his and he knew that whatever Rose was feeling as she stared up at the night sky, he did not feel the same. He had a sense of separation, of dislocation from the ground on which he was treading. Each step was another man's step; each breath was another man's breath. As he crouched for air under a tree, those familiar sensations of his hands and feet moving like snails, while the ground, his face and the sounds of cicadas and frogs rushed like rockets towards him. He found no respite and started jogging around the church.

He moved easily at first then felt compelled to run, to try and keep pace with the objects racing towards him. He ran, his breath at first in rhythm with his legs, but as his thoughts raced ahead of him, his breathing quickened. He lay down and breathed in the cold air from the earth, searching for something to quieten his panic. He ran, then he walked, he lay down, then he ran again. He could find no respite. If he only he could stop, then the world would stop with him. He could only stop and only make the world stop with him by taking his own private steps to end everything. If he stopped breathing, his thoughts would stop tormenting him.

Chapter Sixteen

The army had placed armed barricades at key points around town, encircling the market and the bus stand and providing armed protection for the municipal offices and the District Commissioner. The bus stand being encircled also meant that the army controlled all coach traffic coming in and out of the town. As buses were arbitrarily blocked, most of the bus companies within the first twenty-four hours, stopped their services. Goods lorries did the same. Mbulu was effectively cut off from the rest of the country, something which Babu Jackson amongst others had predicted.

"The phone network will be next, you'll see."

Jackson and Anna and Rose and Noah were in Anna's house. Jackson's house was nearer the market, the other side of the army's barricades. Rose's house was thought too remote. Better be amongst neighbours at Anna's house.

"I tried to phone Father Gerold to see if he is OK. Perhaps Innocent is with him still. There was no answer."

"If he was concerned," said Rose ruefully, "he'd have made his way here to see us."

It was Saturday evening and town was unusually quiet. Normally one district or another throbbed with the beat of speakers hired for a wedding or an anniversary. Bars were empty, stalls selling street food, closed. The huge tapestry of stalls selling cloth, jewellery, shoes, CDs, football shirts, clothes pegs, hair products, sizzling prawns, toothpaste, samosa or cooking oil was unlit, closed. Some traders were by their stalls. They exchanged terse greetings with their neighbours. Samweli and Ali leaned against their wooden stall,

"Oh, my friend. I have a bad feeling. What will this night bring? I have prayed that it would not come to this."

As they talked, a group of youths mostly wearing T-shirts, old football strips, tight blue jeans and rubber sandals marched or danced down the centre of the road, past the street stalls, banging sticks and an old skin drum.

"This is where the trouble will start. The soldiers will try and pick out a few of those noisy ones, the ringleaders."

"I think some of those boys are from out of town. I don't recognise quite a number of them."

Samweli and Ali considered following the growing number marching down the main street.

"Not for me, man" said Ali. "I'll go home. Inshallah, peace will break out and I'll see you tomorrow."

Some people believed they were going to speak to the District Commissioner to ask him to lift the blockade of buses and lorries. Many were expecting relatives from Dar or further afield and were worried. Other believed that this march would help the town with its demands to have the government reopen discussions with the Chinese over the cement factory. Those residents who stayed at home, bolted their doors and left their lights off knew that these young men with the whistles and the drums wanted to fight. They also knew that the soldiers would never allow these young boys to win.

Rose and Anna were sitting together watching Noah close his eyes. Jackson had walked across town to see a friend. The women hoped Noah would sleep. As Rose rocked him, Anna made a small crib on the floor from her blanket and a wooden crate. As Rose stood to lift the baby into the crib, the night sky lit like day. The darkness of their home, even through the small windows, was lit with a white flash. Perhaps two seconds passed, during which time Rose and Anna were able to see each other's faces, and then a crack as loud as thunder but with a higher pitch, like a great tree snapping, hurt their ears and small pieces of mud from the walls near the window fell away. There was another moment's silence. Rose wrapped Noah more tightly in a small blanket while Anna went to the door.

"Come away, Mama. Keep the door closed."

"That sounded like a bomb. Are we at war?"

As she opened the door the night came alive to the sound of sirens, blaring horns and gunshots.

"Lie down," Anna turned to Rose and shouted. "Lie down. A neighbour told me last year that a young girl was killed by a stray bullet. It came right through the house. Lie down."

"Why are they shooting here? We are so far from

town." Rose was trembling, trying to calm Noah and relieved that she was with Anna.

"I don't know."

They heard a vehicle driven at speed. It roared past their house, stopped and then men's voices,

"Go! Go! Each and every house. Drag everyone out if necessary."

Women's voices and children's cries replaced the man's harsh voice.

"Out! Out!", a man's voice that sounded only a few feet away, made Rose grip her baby even more tightly. The door then shook. Anna tried to release the bolt but the door flew back away from her hand. A soldier, quite tall, very young and with a shiny metal gun stooped through the doorway and moved quickly through each of the three rooms.

"Outside! Both of you. Now!"

They stood, Noah in Rose's arms, for thirty minutes, while the soldiers went to every house. They arrested two men and sped off in their jeeps. After an hour, the night seemed as quiet as before. They had to look at the broken lock on their door to remember that ten soldiers had that very evening invaded their small hamlet.

In town, the explosion that had rocked the town had been the spur for General Nchia, commanding officer for this operation, to begin the phase of arrests to find the extremist ringleaders. Dozens of men were arrested and when the police jail was full, they were locked in the army's personnel carriers. Samweli and

Ali, making their way home, took shelter at the first explosion and were then stopped by police and arrested. All those held would stay in custody until Monday or until they could be interrogated by officers and a decision taken as to whether they posed a security threat.

At midnight, Jackson was still sitting on a plastic chair in the clearing near Anna's house discussing the night's events with some of Anna's neighbours.
"The DC is saying that three people have been killed. I don't know where this will end," Jackson's voice was as strong and confident as ever. His thoughts were of uncertainty and violence. He looked at the group of men sitting with him, Muslim and Christian. He understood the differences; in truth, he would have been unhappy had Rose wanted to marry a Muslim. Equally his friend and neighbour of many years would have been troubled had his daughter married a Christian. But it happened. Their generation had passed. A younger generation did not consider these things to be as important. Only last year a student at the college where Rose worked had married a Christian. How they will raise their children, he didn't know but he was becoming wise enough to understand that because he didn't know didn't mean it wouldn't be solved.

Of much greater importance was the abuse of power by the government and its officials. Jackson was well connected and prided himself in nurturing good relations with those in authority. But he was a minnow. And what chance did the ordinary residents of Mbulu stand. Every few years there were elections. At each election, the People's Party won by a big majority, but then once in power, the same People's Party ensured that it gave land and good jobs to its best supporters. Everyone knew that if you wanted a form signing, if you wanted a land issue to go through smoothly, if you wanted promotion at work, then you should be a visible supporter of the Party, or at least be very friendly with someone who was.

The latest conflict, supposedly with Chinese investors, was more than likely a decision of the government to put the factory somewhere else. A Minister or an MP having been bribed, the factory most probably would be built – perhaps in a year or two – in another region. Mbulu would be forgotten again.

Once the gunfire and the noise of jeeps and the blaring horns had stopped Rose took Noah back to her own house. Anna feared that she might lose her footing in the dark but Rose knew the paths well and could use the light on her phone where the moon's shadows made the way too dark to see. She slept little, but was comforted by Noah's deep breaths, his legs as they wriggled and pressed against her belly and the fusty smell in the folds of his chubby flesh. She slept little and was awake with the cockerel. She must have slept a little because she woke with a start and thought of Innocent. Washed and dressed in minutes she made her way back to her mother's house and called in a hoarse whisper from outside,

"Are you awake? I'm going to church. Will you come with me?"
From her voice Rose, knew her mother was still half asleep,
"I'll go to the later Mass. I need to sleep more."
Rose pressed on with Noah on her back and saw a small group of people near the church from some distance. It was early and she could see from the noise they were making that they had not come to Mass. She approached slowly and when she could see some of their faces she stepped off the track and out of sight in the shrubs and small trees.

It was still early. Rose had not looked at the time until after she'd left home, but there was still an hour before the first Mass, so few people would be passing here so early. The church and its grounds were fenced with wire supported by concrete pillars. The fence was shrouded in fast growing ivy and shrubs. It gave the church and its grounds a verdant border causing the compound to stand proud and prevent anyone seeing in other than through the gates. Two large gates padlocked at night were normally unlocked about now, by the night-watchman.

It was unclear what had happened to the night-watchman. Perhaps the night's troubles had meant that he was away from church. He had probably gone to his own family to protect them. Rose was unsure, but the church and its gates remained locked and a group of some five or six people were rattling the gates shouting for them to be opened. She considered running back to town for help but where would she go? Soldiers were everywhere and she would most likely be stopped again and travelling alone made her feel vulnerable. She edged forward from her hiding place. She was now quite visible had the group of people at the fence turned to see. She could now hear some words and see more clearly that these people were not young militants. She moved forward more confidently. As she approached, she heard the group calling,

"Open the gates man"

"It's awful. We can't leave it like this. Where's the priest?"

Rose pressed forward to the locked gates. She saw immediately what had caused the small group of citizens such alarm. To one side of the compound stood a mature flame tree; its thick boughs provided shade in the afternoon for catechists and bible study groups to meet. Tied in a loop round one broad branch was a blue nylon washing line. Swinging from the rope was Innocent's lifeless body, hanging by his neck.

Chapter Seventeen

Innocent's mother came to the funeral but was happy for Jackson to make the arrangements. Father Gerold of course led the service, a simple burial, not Mass, which few people attended. The town was still in the grip of an occupation by the army; there were still outbreaks of violence from Muslim youths and many people felt superstitious about being too close to the body of someone who'd killed themselves. He was buried at the end of the small garden Gerold had created behind his house by the church. To bury him in the cemetery would mean getting special permission from the bishop which would take time and not necessarily be granted. Few people would care if a simple wooden cross marked a patch of earth hidden behind Father Gerold's cassava trees.

Father Gerold surprised a lot of people by dedicating the whole of the following Sunday's homily to the need to look to our closest and dearest and look for signs of those suffering what he called inner trauma. Mental illness was not something understood and certainly not discussed in homes in Mbulu. Most people knew that great sadnesses and fears could take over a person's mind but they were more likely to seek the help of a traditional healer, believing it to be the work of an evil spirit. Gerold did not attempt to explain the cause of such inner trauma, but called on his congregation to look for signs of loneliness, sadness or inexplicable behaviour and to be quick to act and slow to judge.

Rose listened to Father Gerold's sermon intently, understanding every word very personally. It was as though he was talking directly to her. She had been slow to act and quick to judge, wanting, since they were at school, to direct Innocent rather than listen to him. Many aspects of Innocent's life – the mistakes he seemed to make – she knew she couldn't have controlled, but she doubted whether the feeling of guilt that sank deep into her bones and belly would ever escape her.

She pulled Noah's little body closer to her. His chubby hands pawed at her face and her breasts. He had his father's oily black skin and broad nose; in fact, she had few of Rose's, or Anna's or Jackson's features. He was a big baby, with Innocent's feet, broad and strong, like paddles. For a young boy to grow up without a father was not unusual in Mbulu, but Rose understood well from her own experience how much Noah would miss.

Soon after the funeral and more significantly after another night of explosions and gunfire, Jackson suffered a minor heart attack. He was cared for well at the district hospital and returned home a week later. Rose persuaded him that he was too frail to live alone. He refused to move to Anna and, privately, Anna was relieved. Instead, he agreed to move into the small room in Rose's house. His bed and his furniture would not fit into the tiny room but he had enough money to have a bed made that would fit.

Some days after he had completed the move, he sat in the shade of the tree some yards from the house. He held Noah on his knee and told him stories of great battles fought and lost and won; of struggles with lions and leopards; of tensions and relations between tribes that had existed since the days of King Shaka. There was no mention in his stories of World Wars or America or the United Nations. Noah's chubby body struggled to free itself from his great grandfather's bony grip. He'd spotted a scrawny cat in the undergrowth that was stalking Rose's hens. He toddled within a few feet of the cat before the cat quickly moved and took up a position of stealth again. Each time the cat moved, Noah yelped in delight.

Printed in Great Britain
by Amazon